Nick Oliveri

A LETTER FROM THE CONJURER

A Letter From The Conjurer

Nick Oliveri

A LETTER FROM THE CONJURER

A NOVEL BY NICK OLIVERI

Cover design by Aaron Kapuscinski

Nick Oliveri

The conception of this work justifies its own existence. Its every word is imperious. Its every question is a command, and every tear is a true one.

This work will live forever
as I die, as you do too.
But when you read this letter,
be it only me and you.

Laughter silences the freaks inside you, the lurking monsters in your mind you don't want anyone to hear. The louder you laugh, the deeper the evil.

Nick Oliveri

Prologue

A silver dagger gleamed on a lone table. Lustrous sunlight shone through the wide windows of a house. The walls were all white, and the giant room held high ceilings. The dainty dagger on the table lay still, carved with perfectly symmetrical etchings of patterns and eagles and what looked like a family crest.

A man with a dark mane of hair stood there silent. He had a sharp jaw underlying sad eyes that fixated on the lone dagger lying still on the table. Then, something moved in the corner of his eye—a shy flicker formed in the image of a woman he knew. She had long dark hair and smart-sharp eyes. Her long arms were crossed as tightly as her jaw clenched. She looked away through some golden window, imagining some other world she wished existed outside the walls of the mansion.

As the dagger sat still, the man, dressed in a flashy purple robe with gold frills glowing, ran to the woman with arms out wide. "*Jani*! Jani! Jani…." He could finally smile if he could only hold her one last time.

The man brought her body close to his, nudging her face like all those old times. "Your cheek is so cold."

Jani remained unmoved with her arms crossed. Her face soured at the man's embrace, despite his handsome face. She looked away and tilted slightly to a colder posture, one unwilling to give anything to anybody. And so, his only love stayed so painfully close, yet infinitely out of reach.

He thirsted for an imaginary nectar, one he could never have, one branch too high to reach and too stubborn to let its fruits fall. No matter how hard he gripped the brown branch or kicked the tree's trunk, the fruit wouldn't fall into his palm. And his stomach so hungered for that final peach, with a grip on the fortified fuzz, biting slowly into hard skin that softened in the sun. And he begged and pleaded with the tree when his body's force couldn't knock the fruit off the branch. It wasn't enough. It would never be enough. The only one he wanted could never be his; that sacred lone tree ignored him for all time. He only looked at the fruit and admired the beauty of the tree in its infinite glory; he knew he'd put it all in a story, the itch in the base of his spine twitching, twisting his face into tears. He would talk about the spark that started by rubbing the exhilaration of life with his desire for death. Sparks—they burned his eyes.

"Jani… what's wrong? It's me, Mikalla.…"

Her voice was soft. "You're dead, Miki." She pulled away a slight bit more. Her fingertips drifted off his body. Her torso slightly jerked away from his. She pulled back from his body—only a few inches—but enough distance to carve a deeper crater in his chest. He once felt so full just with the thought of her. It was all empty lust and rotting flesh he imagined his rib cage contained.

"I don't care what I am. I care where I am—and *that's with you*. You know that.… My Love, you know that. I know you do." The man realized that the fireplace in the room was cold and barren, and the woman gave off no heat. He shivered. He shriveled. He felt like his insides were darker than night clouds, deeper than the void in a bleak world.

Jani took a deep breath. She eyed the dagger and looked all around the vast white walls. She pressed her lips tightly and leaned away from the man. "I know, Miki... I know you love me. I know you want me and only me. All your life, you've enchanted millions with stories of gods and goddesses, mythical stories that have captured... the hearts of everyone you've encountered." She gulped, trying to shimmy out of the man's hold on her. "But I know I'm *your* goddess. I am your true goddess, and you've spent a great part of your life worshiping me, working for my approval, even fighting for your life just to impress me."

Mikalla loosened his grip. "What are you trying to say? You know you're my only, Jani. I love you and always have. The great heavens and the ultimatum of the universe have driven me straight to you…. And I love you. I love you so hopelessly, boundlessly, and powerlessly. I love you existentially. I love you physically. I love freely. I love you as if my soul were stamped for your custody before it ever entered this damned world we both called home."

Jani tried to tune his words out, but they echoed all around her and sang out to her soul.

She was the youngest of six in a royal family. She always ate the finest food, donned the best dress, and walked on soft green grass ever since she was young. She had only ever been touched by fine linens, but never embraced by her father's fine hand.

She thought back to a time as a child. It was a rare occasion when her father returned home from his responsibilities as the High Priest of Idaza. The little girl with long dark hair felt a rush of joy and excitement at the thought of sitting on her father's lap, feeling the touch of his cheek and the embrace of his arms. But while running toward her daddy, she was tripped by her older brother and tumbled onto a stone floor with only her little wrist to break her fall. She heard the echoes of her father laughing and playing with her older siblings somewhere far off in the sun. The only thing her childish eyes could see were vast empty halls and a reddened, broken wrist—alone, abandoned, tossed aside because she lost the footrace to affection. Through tears and grit teeth, the little girl vowed that she would never be tripped up again. Instead, she promised herself to always be one step ahead—ahead of her peers, her siblings, her lovers, and anyone else that got in her way.

She couldn't overpower her older brothers. She couldn't outsmart her older sisters. Instead, she had to outwork and keep her heart as cold and hard as the stone she fell on that long time ago.

And so, she pulled away from Mikalla. The man let go and pulled his cheek away from hers.

"We had a son, Jani." Mikalla turned his head and tried to hold the tears. "We had love…. We had youth. We had a *family*! We had everything."

Jani turned away. Even from the back, Mikalla could never mistake her beauty, the contours of her sonsy body always drew him in. And, looking away, a lone tear rolled down his cheek. Somewhere and at some time—in the distant life he remembered—he lost Jani to a different force. She was no longer his. And before the spears stabbed him as he stood on top of the world, he realized that he never had anything with Jani. He never had her at all.

Mikalla eyed the silver dagger with the mahogany handle. He knew it to be Jani's knife, the only family heirloom she had—and it was a royal weapon, engraved with her powerful family crest and polished with a veneer that shone so bright it seemed to sparkle by the light, shaped like a sharp thunderbolt.

All of Mikalla's memories connected and culminated in a lone, tragic tear that left his eye and slid down his cheek.

Silence set between them. It hung like a cloud. The light in the room suddenly blinded Mikalla and stung his salty eyes.

"If you care about me, if only a little, Jani, then grab that knife and kill me with it. Kill me so I can bleed by you. I want to be a martyr for a cause that cares not for me. Stab me and slice me, Jani, with your family's knife. It wouldn't be the first time your family's hurt me, but I want it to be the last."

Mikalla cleared his throat as his tear dried and looked at the floor. Jani remained still and despondent, clutching at the depths of her hardened heart, trying her best to ignore Mikalla's words. She still had power over him, and just as she'd never let go of her lonely childhood, so would she never let go of the iron grasp she had on her husband's bleeding heart.

"I want to thank you, Jani—not for the things you've done for me…. In fact, you've done very little to support me or please me with favors or loving words or... really, anything. But I do have to thank you. I want to thank you for what you've shown me. I see your pain, Jani, not just your pretty face. I see the truth in your eyes. I see your past in your lies. You taught me that I can love something and someone that may never love me back. You taught me a love so pure, so universal, so true, to a depth I could have never known without you. And it hurts me to say this and face it." Mikalla looked defeated at the ground with bleak eyes. "But without lack, there is nothing—no life, no love, no matter, nothing. And because of you, your lack of love for me... *my life mattered*. You never shackled me. You *freed* me, Jani. You freed me into an existence of pain and desire, two things that make a boundless life worth living, and two things that make stories worth spreading. You made me. You, *you* did this! You sculpted me into something that even strikes fear into the hearts of the gods.

Now, I want you to undo me. I want you to dismantle me so I could die a death worth living and bleed by something that was never there. And yet I loved you all the same. I want to die by eternal love—the passion of absence and abandonment. I want to die by you."

Mikalla's dark eyes looked toward the dagger on the table. He waved his hand toward it.

Jani stared at the man who had clearly gone mad, in a strange realm where she only had him to talk to for some reason. Her bewildered look turned to astonishment, then fear, then chaos, as her face morphed to all sorts of horror and loathing. She realized that she was again, even after life, trapped—utterly trapped. But this crazed man she recognized all too well—*his weak emotional little spells, being dramatic as usual. Little weak man who thinks his mind is all that great, trying to manipulate me? Of all people, he thinks he can trick me? After all these years, he's remained the same—a weak little man who should bow to me and be spit on for doing so.*

"Take the dagger, Jani. The one—*that* one—on the table. Take that dagger and drive it into me. Slice me with it for the first and last time. Hurt me like you always have."

Jani looked at the broken man. She eyed the gleaming weapon. Her hand twitched. She twisted her face. Eyebrows locked in place, making wrinkles and folds in her skin that showed the conflict within her.

"Kill me with it. Do it how you like but do it fast."

Jani just stood there in place, twitching and shivering under her satin robes. She'd lied and cheated in her life. But she had never killed anyone—at least, not yet.

Chapter 1

A Drunken Man Sits Atop The World

A young man overlooked an entire city from a rocky perch above, surrounded by wistful green grass underneath open air and tranquil skies, listening to a chorus of crickets. He wore a ratty brown cloak with a hood that sloped over his forehead and covered his sharp, watchful eyes. He inhaled the rich air of rare and scarce peaks and sat on a boulder on the top of a mountain peak that overlooked all of it.

***

Surely, the young man wanted to change what he looked at from above. But what young person doesn't wish to change the world for the better?

But this was not merely some young man with a charming face and a silver pen that wanted things to be different, people to be better, streets to be cleaner, and more money given to the poor. This was a man who was crazy enough to think he could actually do it all and change it all, no matter what it would take. He was unafraid, made less cowardly by his trials as a boy. For a time, it felt like the only thing he knew was how to lose the things and people closest to him. His life to that point was like gripping a block of ice in his warm palm, wishing it would stay in his hand if he only gripped harder. Maybe—*maybe*—next time the ice wouldn't melt if he'd only had a stronger grip! But he had nothing much else left to grasp for in his own tiny life. All of that was gone.

And that would make him a danger soon enough to all those around him. His dagger would flash the most. His fire would burn the brightest. Looking down on the present city, he saw the work of past generations. He didn't care about any of the old men of the past, any of the old wars, and paid no reverence to the marble sculptures of the "*heroes*" that the nobility praised constantly.

***

He saw it all from far away—everyone working, living, and trying to do their very best for themselves and their families. The only peace he felt was when the rush of the city streets could no longer be heard. High up on the mountain, he could even see the Inner Gardens in the center of the city, surrounded on all sides by the massive sprawl of commons. Most nobles thought the commoners to be dirty and vulgar. They were wrong. It was actually the nobles, in all their glitz and gleaming dress, may very well have been dirtier than any commoner at heart. Their pompous, decadent ways could not have been blamed on them solely, though, for their souls were so tainted at the very outset of their birth from a genealogy of power and hunger for more and more and more of it.

Maybe it mattered.

Coyote saw through the dresses and robes and smiles, and he figured that the noble people were just as fallible, just as broken as every one of the commoners, except they'd just been given more at birth—more money, nicer clothes, more wine, and fancier parties with fine linens and satin garments and delicate chalices.

The man in the ratty brown cloak watched over all of them. They were all beautiful—infinitely different. And yet, they were all bound by the same things.

Coyote came from a wealthy and powerful family of the greatest influence, yet he lived in the dirt for a long while and was formed by the slums of grit and grime. He made the danger of the rusty dagger his home. The filth of trash comforted him. He used the ragged scraps of the streets as a thin blanket. But no blanket could warm him in the cold, black night. His splotches of loose, bumped skin hardened with the wind. His jaw grinded like running rocks while his face sagged as if he grew decades older in minutes of time. The memory of endless sands of dumb desert hills shook his body in the heat—relentless lashings from uncaring people.

He flinched when he thought about all the lashings that struck him as a boy on the run from something he didn't understand. But now he understood it.

His bare skin stuck with ripe red infractions running with blood. And his blood was holy, just like any animal. He was a lamb to the slaughter, as the decadent nobles wanted and wished for him to be.

But this lamb, this young man with a strong jaw and sharp eyes—he never got slaughtered. He was the son of the kingdom. He was the son of The Last Conjurer. The son of suffering. A child—never meant to grow old— raised by the dirt, never feeling at home even while living out his years in the house he grew up in.

The guards of foreign kingdoms wanted to hurt him. They tried their best with their spears, chains, and whips.

But he found his purpose in running away from it all. He was born into something he was meant to do. But he was also meant to run away from what he was born into. It was part of a process he'd never understand.

He'd seen sadness. Dead bodies were nothing to him. He'd seen piles of them. What cut him, though, was a broken soul in a living body; there was nothing more devastating than a life without a purpose. Sallow eyes, sunken heads, broken backs, twisted minds, dead souls in live bodies.

But against the endless pits of evil and sin, the young man's short life yielded rich returns of fervor and pure anguish—a roaring death that screeched to the heavens. Guttural and grim presences were what he lived among for so long.

The boy was okay with living hellish nightmares. He'd already done so, and why be afraid of things that have already hurt you?

As young men often do, Coyote thought that he'd seen it all. As he looked down upon the gigantic metropolis that other forefathers built, he felt he knew everyone in the city—intimately. He thought he'd been through everything there was to be through. And was he ever wrong? Had he ever been so wrong in his tiny life?

See, from up top, he saw it all—everyone and everything that went on in the entire kingdom. But the further away one stood, the less one got to feel. A person's clever mind took over when they stood far away from anything. They just thought about statistics and ideas. But the abstract and cerebral mind was no match for the experience of the body as it got bruised and starved.

The cold young man in the cheap brown cloth only got to see the movement of the city from some high and away place. He really knew nothing. His head only told him lies—he thought he'd felt the extent of suffering. He thought he'd been through it all.

But Oh! There was so much more to go through. There were so many more lonely streets to traipse through.

And there was so much more to be saddened about. And there were still corners of life to rejoice in.

That's what he failed to realize as he stood on the mountain, far away and above the millions of common people that scuttled in the race of life. Alone.

He was no better than them. He was just one of them, just as they were of him. He didn't have royal blood. He was not born significant. He quickly sifted to dust as the memory of his father faded fast in the many fickle minds of the kingdom.

But his words did things to the kingdom he failed to know. His written words that bled from his lone pen also beat and pumped in the hearts of those he looked down upon—the world, even—that he never appreciated.

The commoners forgot why they had markets to begin with. They just worked and traded. When they got their food, they ate it, and when they were told to do something, they did it.

The hooded man glared down at the whole of the kingdom with a love that flooded from his tired heart—tired of losing, tired of caring.

The commoners forgot everything so quickly. The nobles cared so little. They only cared for their next meal. But how easy it would be for that meal to be left behind in the woods, still alive, still running faster than the feeble human foot.

The man's name was Coyote, son of a great man. As he stared down at the kingdom from some nearby mountain peak, he realized something. It was a vicious and glaring thought he wanted to run from. For so long, he actually was able to evade the truth. But in the quiet mist of the mountain peak, breathing in the pine-scented air, Coyote knew one thing: he wanted to be different, wanted to be special, or some sort of savior like he'd heard about in stories passed down from the old king. He wanted his life to mean something—but not just something, *more. He wanted his life to mean more.* More than those on the ground, he peered down from the heights. But if he yelled out to the greater heavens, no one would hear him. If he visited his late father's grave for the thousandth time, only the soil would show on the ground. No spirit would visit him. No God would endow him with a special gift.

And this desire to be special and above others was selfish—he knew that. But if he were selfish, what would it matter? What would another selfish man add to the world? He knew from evil merchants past and present that another selfish hand would only take—take from the earth, from others, from the people that were supposed to trust them.

He didn't know if he cared that he was selfish or not. But he wasn't special. That was certain. He bled like the rest. He cried when sad and ate when hungry. As much as he wished to be some god to be worshiped and praised at every whim, he was none like anything except average and human. He was only fiercely and brutally human. He looked a hairy creature in its bloodshot eyes when he stared into the puddle below him. It reflected a broken man.

And so, looking down on a city of ants—some poor, some rich—what was his calling? His father was just another dead person. The stupid boy thought the world needed his father, The Conjurer. He thought the kingdom needed The Conjurer to give the markets their money and the warriors their spears—their reason for being. But looking down, way down, at the people and their meaningless work toward meaningless tasks, it didn't seem to be any story or myth that motivated the people. An individual could still exist in the collective.

An individual could still exist in a group.

Or could it? Could this story itself even serve to move anyone, and if so, what difference would that movement make?

If one killed one, and if one killed many, what would we be left with the one who killed? If all would be ash one day, what did a gold coin mean today?

The man named Coyote had shed too many tears in his youth to cry on top of the mountain. Maybe all he needed was peace. But no mind achieves peace when burdened with these types of questions. No single thing sits still on Earth. Even the emperor changed with the seasons.

The man with the oversized brown hood sat on a fat gray rock. He grumbled and took a big gulp of red wine. The red river of drink was as good as gold. But the wine felt good; on the mountain, sitting on the rock, the deep red spirit felt nice and warm in Coyote's stomach. It burned the insides of the man, melting away the hard lines of his vision and the edges of his harsh thoughts. Every living person from way below now looked like an ant, an insect, a tiny and insignificant organism. Coyote left the blissful state of the wine as he continued to swig and swig and drink the wine down to its amber glass bone. He soon turned a little angry and restless on his seat from way up high.

The grizzled man soon got up and started to pace; his face then turned away from the city and toward the endless misty horizon. He looked on at the delving sun setting for the millionth time—on the kingdom, his life, his plans that started and changed with each day.

He stared at the night sky instead of looking at his own future, for his 'future' was bleak and blurred, not knowing what to do next after he was fed and clothed. He knew nothing of what to do or who to influence. If he could sway one mind of the kingdom, then what would he do with that heart, that child, or that person? He didn't need money. More gold in his pocket would have meant more options with all the same boring endings.

In his blinding drunken state, he sought hardship. He figured it was the icy thrill of challenge that made any conquest worth the struggle and weight of the human soul. The more he explored—the city, other people, and even his own soul—the less he seemed to know about science, art, and industry.

Was it really necessary to know Hell in order to appreciate Heaven?

Was it really necessary to know Hell in order to appreciate Heaven?

The drunk man cared to know but didn't care enough to find out. They were all idiots to him. But he was no tyrant—he considered himself chief among all idiots. But he knew he was no better than them. If anything, by his own definitions, he was a worse person than most he'd ever met.

Clutching an empty bottle of wine, he just shrugged as a lonely man on top of the world.

And who cared that he sat atop the mountain? Who cared that he was clothed and fed and drunk and rich if he was alone with no one to enjoy it all with him?

And he laughed. Yes, at the top of the mountain on high, looking at his subjects, he cackled like a sick hyena. Laughter silences the freaks inside you, the lurking monsters in your mind you don't want anyone to hear. The louder you laugh, the deeper the evil. He laughed like a mighty lion.

No one. No one cared. And did he care? Who cared about that? He didn't. And that attitude, twisted by a life of strife, did not care for the opinions of the many.

Girls. Slender figures that stared from afar with cat eyes looking to bring him into their chaotic orbit of claws and carcasses, collecting their piles of carnage for their own pleasure of their visions of more. But what were worldly pleasures to the man at the top of the mountain? Sitting on the top of an entire society for more than a moment made a man more worthless than the lowest laborer. What was Coyote's position anymore? If not toiling in the dirt or being beaten by angry guards, what did his life mean? And it was that: the meaning he pursued that so quickly evaded him like the invisible wind at the top of a lonely peak. If he needed other people for a place to stay—a place to belong—then what was his life now, taking cold walks to lofty heights, breathing rare air, seeing from places where no one else was able to? It all seemed as lonely as the dust his sandals stamped.

What was an achievement if he could not brag about his toil to get there, to achieve that long-sought statue?

Coyote's stupid thoughts left him while he drained the wine from his lone bottle into his purple mouth. The cold air of the settling night numbed his body. The deep kiss of the purple potion dimmed his soul. He could even smile for a second as he watched his thoughts melt away.

He climbed to the top just to be bored and alone.

He toiled at the bottom of the streets, beaten and spat on, only to have no one to hold him, no soul to cling to on a spiraling journey to cold nowhere, a barren plain.

His jumbled thoughts clung to a single question:

What if I need a higher power?

If his father's myths were made from mere human hands, were there any gods that could call upon their people and be truly heard?

What if I need a higher power?

Thoughts rolled as thunder did, clapping around his head so loud he couldn't hear his empty amber bottle smash against the jagged boulder. Chunks of glass flew everywhere.

He stood up with sunken eyes that had seen much and a stomach emptier than his mind. He stumbled down the hill and watched the sun paint its pink strokes in drunken double vision as he made his way back down to the kingdom.

The wine helped to keep his mind from thinking as he descended down the hill. The night grew colder, and he stumbled some more, tripping and tumbling over a rock. He got up and didn't care to check his arms or face for scrapes. He needed those people of Idaza, and he'd return to them, as he did, time and time again.

The sun rested again after it laid its new picture out for all to see. Coyote was then just one of the crowd. He looked like a poor drunk in a ratty cloak. The controlled murmurs of the streets buzzed louder as he submerged back into the soft symphony of society.

There would be more pain than a simple scrape to come. *Why can't I just be happy? I can't be happy, though—I want to be great. But what is that?*

Chapter 2

The Kingdom Dies

King Oro's life had entered its final chapter. Much wine had been chugged, and many feelings stuffed deep inside, willing to wither what was left of his insides. Time ticked away. Death smiled at the people who avoided their final arrival, crying above the dirt as if there were no awaiting grave.

The king coughed up flecks of blood. Alone, he had no more trusted advisers—he'd had all his courtiers killed. His twitching eye stared at a twisted world in constant change, slowly melting into a pile of flesh all working as one. Hard walls of a gray chamber surrounded the shriveling old man; his bedsheets were thin and loose over his cold body. His jolly gut shrank over the years; he deflated into a sallow and pale man with loose skin and less smile. The lone man who'd always yearned to carry his family's proud legacy failed to ever have children. He had no heir. The legacy ended with him, and he knew that. His ancestors glared down on the pathetic boy who couldn't continue the line after a millennium of fighting and forcing their way into a kingdom of rich history and hard marble and blue skies.

The last remembrance of the rich Menizak legacy rested in the cold gray eyes of King Oro. As he lay dying, his eyes, his wistful face and shallow breath—all of him—resembled his father when he looked upon the world for the last time. Both men held the same cold, marble-gray eyes—the death of two lives so different looked the same in the end.

Yes, the cold gray eyes of the dead were the only family heirlooms passed down from Menizak The Great, the father of Oro's grandfather. And now, the lineage lived faintly in the eyes of the last one. All who came before this dying king were known for something—their faces were beloved to the embracing public. Oro's royal lineage was a great, lionized family that had made its mark on world history, building an empire of marble and gold, a great beacon to be worshiped. And the bloodline stopped with him. His gray eyes that clung to life were so cold—a rare type of frigid freeze that rattled whatever beats inside bones, frosting over a slowing body.

Things used to be so simple, Oro thought. *Craftsmen used to be just craftsmen. Soldiers were loyal to only the king. Commoners were poor laborers, and nobles were cultured legislators that cared. That's always how it was—what my father knew, and even what his father knew. What happened? I guess now everybody has the taste of gold lining their thirsty tongue... and that rich taste doesn't wear off quickly... no, no. And now, our workers don't want to work; our soldiers would rather stay safe than risk their lives for the sake of their kingdom. Idaza has softened into clay. And I presided over it, watched it happen, even made it so.*

The gray king coughed. His sunken stomach convulsed violently on the bed as the sound of his hacking chest echoed off lifeless walls. So much had happened, and the poor rich man had done so much, and yet his life still seemed like a blurry dream. He reminisced about tumultuous times. He looked back on back stabbings, betrayal, and killing rats in his cabinet. And now he couldn't trust a soul except for his adopted son. He put his last bit of fleeting faith in a young man, but still a boy in his eyes. But his last hope in his storied legacy—who Oro thought to be the lifeline of the kingdom—insisted on wearing smelly brown robes and growing his beard out as something of a sad, drifting vagabond. That man was his last, dying hope. And, in Oro's mind, the last hope of the kingdom. The most painful thing, though, was nothing in his dying body but the doubts in his mind about the young man who lost his way, the last tether to bridge the next generation of something he couldn't understand, held by a boy he still didn't feel like he fully knew.

The king could so easily have gotten attacked and stabbed by someone close to his chambers. He was defenseless, and, for the first time in his life, *he didn't care that he was vulnerable*. He didn't care that his sore and limp body was open to any threat with a dagger and a dream.

King Oro yelled as best he could through his dusty old throat. It hurt his insides to yell, straining his chest and tearing his stomach.

"Guard. Guard!" He coughed and hacked away, calling for some assistant he no longer trusted inside dark palace halls where walked shadowy figures he didn't seem to know. "Guard! *Guard*!"

A tall, muscled man in all red ran into the room and faced the sickly king with a concerned look. He kneeled down and closed his eyes. "My King, what may I do for you?"

"Bring in the boy." The king wheezed. "Coyote. Bring in my boy."

"We will fetch him and have him in your room as soon as possible."

"Do it sooner than possible."

"It will be done, Your Highness."

The guard stood above the bed for a single moment and screwed his face in pity for the old man. It was all a dying shell. Maybe some life somewhere would be born again. But the guard didn't think much about the cycle of life and rebirth. He just watched and felt sad.

***

The bearded man felt an odd sense, as if eyes were intently fixed upon him.

As his old leather boots made their way toward silent crowds, more ants doing their jobs, he voiced out questions to the ghouls that may or may not have surrounded him. "Hello? Hello? Anyone there?" His voice rang out in the empty air.

But it must've been his imagination.

But he really thought he heard a jealous rock jumble right near him.

He swiveled his head and held his breath. His heart thudded, and his drunken double vision sharpened. His instincts took over, narrowing his ears to anything that sounded soft enough to want to hide.

"Hello?"

The wine made him look clumsy and crazy to onlookers he passed by. He scrambled down narrow alleyways and ran down paths quicker as the hum of the noisy kingdom seeped into the dark wind. He ran then crept, but his steps were shaky and tilted like his vision. The people he passed by sneered at him and avoided his stinking presence. *Another homeless person*, they thought. *Our city's really going down the drain.* They all sneered at the dirty man with the hidden face.

Finally, he forgot about being followed, as his body thirsted for rest that night. He learned to love the night and its stillness yet grew to hate that indifferent buzz of endless laborers and traders that got in the way of the peaceful calm of the dark. People always working, toiling away. Markets became crowded again after some time in the dark era of thieves and evils.

And why were they born?

And why did they have to work just to feed their family?

Why did they have families anyway?

No one asked to be born—or so I think.... I didn't, anyway.

Coyote decided, after so many years and pain, that he could never answer these questions. *It was all watered down now, anyway*, he thought. His teeth slid and grinded in his mouth as he approached his house. It was the home he was raised in all those years ago, jumping into his father's arms and nuzzling his head into his mother's bosom. It was taken from him long ago when he was orphaned in a fell swoop. The wine helped him live in his house and forget those good times of the past, those bad times of the past. For a long time—a cold and lonely stretch—he could only look towards the mansion as a dark tower looming over the rest of the Inner Gardens like an empty ghoul. But the king granted him his childhood home when he was old enough to live on his own.

It was still just as empty as when he left it when his mother was ruthlessly assassinated. He trashed the carpets and couches stained by his mother's blood. He emptied out most of the mansion, where only he could sit and feel it all rush in. Rush in. The sharp edges of memories of a lost and forgotten child of the wind. Coyote was like anyone else—he only wanted his parents' approval and to live in a community that cared for him.

But that community never came.

His parents never gave him a sign of life beyond death. He only believed them to be corpses dead and decaying as black bodies beneath beautiful graves.

He kept his late parents' room empty—just as he'd left it. He never visited the empty, dark chamber that was once filled with light and love—memories of running and jumping on his parents' bed as a kid, the plush pillows cushioning the impact of his child's body. But that body has since grown—bones hardened with his mind, his eyes and jaw and cheeks sharpened, sculpted by the edges of a dangerous life lived.

His steps now echoed emptily in the vacant mansion. The house seemed to take on a life of its own. He walked up the stairs to the only haven he had left in the world—in front of his desk. It was splattered with all sorts of papers and writings, scribbles snaking all around the space, incoherent ramblings about the cosmos. The large oak desk sat under the mural of a great man, arms raised in a 'V.' The proud man performed for the people of an entire nation with stories from a heart that bled for humanity and all its suffering. He was The Last Conjurer.

And then his ears quivered at a sound in the night. He stopped breathing and jerked his head toward his door.

There it was again, but louder. And louder still.

Coyote tucked his robe and sprung to his feet. He chose not to have guards to defend his home. He thought that if someone powerful wanted him dead, it would have been done already. With that, he rushed down the stairs with a dagger clutched behind his back.

"Hello?"

Knock knock.

"Hello?" Coyote heard a muffled voice through the thick wood of the giant front door.

"I come as a messenger of your king, His Royal Highness."

He widened his eyes and ripped the door open. "What is it?"

"His Highness calls for you now. I suggest you get dressed and—"

"I don't need to get dressed. Take me to him at once!" Coyote said, cutting the messenger off. With no siblings or children, the king proved to be his last lifeline to a painful past. He couldn't escape from the past he clung to. His losses all along the way formed him into the man he was today—for better or for worse.

Coyote had access to half the gold in the world and spent none of it. What would he buy that would be worth anything? He dressed in itchy brown burlap sacks that left his skin red. He walked in bare feet. He let his beard grow long to hide his face and jaw so only his eyes showed. His sharp eyes. His sad eyes. His eyes that'd seen sand and rocks and preying birds eating away at rotting black-smelling flesh.

He ran out of his room with bare feet and barely a thin cloth covering his lean skeletal body. He rushed toward the only man that meant anything to him. Since he stared at the void of death every day, he related to the dying king. He sympathized. Oro may possibly have been the emperor's last tether to humanity.

The bearded man in the ratty brown hood rushed to a place where he thought two lives would end—his and the king's. He no longer held a heart for the kingdom. He no longer believed in people—not even himself. He resented organisms, animals, humans, leaves, and the trees they fell from. Coyote stopped believing in the suffering and light of life.

The light dimmed long ago in the mind of the young, bearded man—you could see the dark clouding his eyes. *But there still existed a spark somewhere deep in the dark.*

As he rushed alongside the king's aide, he noticed the many noble mansions standing high and proud. And what were they proud of? That they were tall and built by males that wanted females? That they were built by women who thirsted for glory and jewels? Any motivation to be wealthy and proud seemed stupid to the man rushing toward the king, his only friend, in a time of dire need.

Coyote reached the palace gates and was let through immediately. The guards knew him too well. They knew Coyote from afar, always watching him, never speaking to him. They knew the bearded man like a young child knew his late grandfather. As long as they were paid, they felt bad for the unkempt kid with wild eyes, somehow rich, somehow unhappy still with his large inheritance.

Everything confused them. The king's guards listened to the king because he paid them. Without coins from the king, they were wolves willing to eat him alive. But while the old man breathed, he still kept the guards and the nobles and the entire kingdom in order. But the whole world hung by a loose string attached to the gray king's coughing heart, his failing body staying alive by a prayer and a few hopeful cells.

The king wasn't even sure why he hung onto life with one foot in the grinning afterlife.

Still, the two had to meet. The kid ran along and wished it weren't the last time he would hold Oro, all the while crying in fear that his hopes were nothing.

Sometimes those that gave orders never cared to rule after all. Most bosses were scared. Most kings only gave orders to feel their mother's touch but never to be graced again by someone who really cared. Oro thought about the people he'd known in his life. There were maybe two that appreciated him with all his flabby flaws and anxious edges; they liked him without a title or without a crown on his head.

But Coyote really cared about this man. Memories throughout his life of a sad, smiling face told stories all their own with no words. This old shell, who was once a proud, laughing lion—the king in the wake of a great legacy—loved Coyote as a son with a heart as large as the sun itself. And the two men shared the same heartstring, the same love for one another—a mentor and his young prodigy. They had love. They clung to life, despite hating life and never finding true love.

It was all they had.

No longer did gold or palaces or banquets or women or fine wine mean *anything* to the gray, dying king. But with every tear he shed alone on his gray bed, he thought about regrets and challenges, and saw the people that passed through his life as only pictures—not real, only visions of a crazy mind. But the king grew to love Coyote as his own son, as his last tether to a cruel world that only served to hate him and despise him for his power over others. Everything Oro did and regretted splattered in and out of his fuzzy head in violent flashes. It seemed that the only time he could think clearly was when he thought about the son of the man he could have saved.

Coyote ran to King Oro with blisters on his feet, a sore back, and tired eyes that always wanted to close. His chest heaved, and he coughed as he ran to his last father figure, as bleak and blackened memories of the past melted around the outsides of his vision. Sometimes, he didn't want to think he had a past. Sometimes, the whole concept of the past was lost on the boy, now a man—the lone coyote that howled while things just simply moved around him.

Simpler times were behind him. For as much he struggled then—the boy of the past in the brown cloak, ragged in the streets, bruised by the guards who hurt him for money—it was only to grow harder.

Lonely roads only go farther.

Coyote stormed past all the palace walls and by the guards that watched his face change and sink over the years. Although he rarely talked, his voice could reach a violent pitch that could chill blood and redden eyes. He yelled.

And he yelled again. The only sound in the entirety of the Inner Gardens—seemingly, in the whole city— came from behind the fangs of an animal, the tired teeth of a man, the wrinkled pink throat of someone who was once a boy.

"Orrrrrrrrrrrrrooooooooooooooooooooo!"

He listened for a yell back, some shout, or even just a weak whimper from a far-off room. He heard nothing. He saw only fine paintings and golden ornaments littered throughout the giant hall. He looked at canvases that seemed to blur and move. Every vase seemed so close to the edge of the tables, ready to fall and crash at any moment.

He crept through the dark palace under a ceiling that stretched to the sky. And yet, it all seemed to be a tiny tunnel. Marble busts and marble floors with no end in sight.

Finally, he heard a voice. "Coyote, His Highness is this way. He's been calling for you all day."

A tiny, lone ache in the young man's chest shriveled at the words of the royal guard.

None of it spelled any good. But what story could only be hopeless? How could this whole arc, this cast of the most unlikely, the most human characters, be only a story that spells no hope?

That couldn't be the case. But the grave never twitched. Only life could yearn for more, and while there was life, there was still hope.

Chapter 3

Children Can't Be Wise Before They're Hurt

The sprawling commons of the city hummed. It was a steady stream of sound, soothing to the ear and electrifying the mind. This was many years after the slanging and banging hammers and yelling merchants and droves of wide-eyed fiends and pale-skinned zombies and children selling and stealing bread in the streets and drunkards binging on powders, liquids, pastes—whatever would tickle their sternum's tired twitch. That old utopia had come and gone. A new future was ushered in by the words of a prophet, the times of a new preference, ushered in by the gentle, harsh, anxious, hateful, loving, heartfelt letters of the faceless boy emperor from somewhere above where they couldn't see or hear him. This was a new age in Idaza, slowly, assuredly, brought forth and fought about, debated and discussed by the masses of the commons ushered in by the pain of the pen of one man they never saw but knew all too well.

The commoners listened to Coyote's words; they weren't sad, but desperate people. You can be desperate and happy. And that was what the people of Idaza were—desperate and happy with wide eyes searching for hope. They were spurred on soullessly by the coca powder. Everyone worked for one man's will. They all got high on the tasks of a higher goal they never knew, enriching a hidden man high up and away from the commons they built themselves. That now-dead man watched the people do his bidding, thinking they were "working for themselves."

He sat on his perch and smiled about the lives he controlled with a coin, the souls he emptied and made shells for speckled metals.

But years after the death of the man—*that man*—the people seemed steadier with smiles all across their many painted faces, working steadily but not without a soulless vigor. They just worked. They were more honest, even when they lied to each other. The people of the commons decorated more things and held more tender joy in their hearts—they twitched less and talked more simply with their neighbors and friends. The people of the kingdom—the many countless commoners—cared more about their own health and the well-being of their friends while still working hard at things they finally sought to understand.

Years and years of peace had arrived, despite all the advancements in weapons and armor. Unlike past times, Idaza's military was not their primary focus. Their people flourished and suffered, smiled through pain, and loved the thrall of a challenge. Somehow, this was the only city—fictional or otherwise or anything else—that struggled every day while still profiting and smiling and making money and expressing themselves in the only way they knew. Money exchanged hands quickly. Art was bought often. Vases, tapestries, and blankets were savored. Their creators were held in high regard in many neighborhoods. Some sort of utopian, magical, heavenly, priceless, and transcendent culture wrapped around the happy and peaceful people of Idaza. Many got rich, yet they didn't take advantage of one another. There were fewer thieves and more repairmen, more smiles, and yet more tears still. The people lived fuller, richer, poorer, and more dangerously than ever. The whole city of millions lived on the knife's edge.

There were still those that lived ragged and dirty, drifting from street to street, finding small solace in dark alleyways. Some went hungry still, and many more middling that worked and could eat comfortably, and yet all seemed to click along with the steady progress of the city.

The commons of Idaza have never seen a sun so bright and vibrant. The colors of Idaza never ran so brightly despite their king's gray, dry skin. But they don't know about that. They didn't care about their king so long as he didn't choke their markets or tax their businesses.

Now, the common streets were no utopia—but they were the perfect setting for suffering and climbing, a brightly burning balance for better things. Vibrant streamers of reds and greens and vibrant royal purples celebrated some freedom never known to the commons. And it wasn't the government that made this. The government made way for a bearded young man that hated shoes and fancy clothes to write, write, and paint the pictures of a better future.

Coyote's stories spread to millions; his words of creativity without a face were the mirrors the people could look into and fear and weep and be happy that it all happened. Crime still existed. Police still existed. But markets flourished quickly before they got depressed, heaving final breaths before dying and rising once more. Creativity and art came from the sadness of people's past and present sorrows, and, instead of ignoring the darkness of life, the nighttime was embraced with a cold flame.

This was a kingdom that no king—not Menizak The Great, his son, his grandson, and certainly not King Oro—could ever institute. State power relied on revenue streams of gold for control, paid to make spears, and then reap more gold from the people who still lived in straw so they could see the stone while giving the king his gold.

Coyote's stories didn't need gold or taxes. The Emperor of Idaza didn't need spears to protect sacred words. His government was not a government at all. His king was ignored; that was the great thing! Art and culture and soldiers and books and food and markets existed in the imaginations of the people of the kingdom. The people. Happy to suffer in sadness, living lives of strife and energy, pain and production to achieve feelings gold could never give them. But no one was sure it would work out. No one was sure when the sun would set on that new age as it dawned before them all.

It was exactly what Coyote wanted for the kingdom, and yet his despair struck him deeply every day, darker every night.

The young man was the foul beast created.

The young man that resurrected the kingdom's belief, the scraggly successor to his great father, wanted to die. Dying—living in the great void of the unknown—he thought of every day. Maybe it would come sooner than expected. But for now, the emperor's tired chest still contained a small spark. And that spark in his heart had a life of its own, seeking tender wood to consume someday.

No matter where that tinder took the spark, it would eat greedily, because that's all sparks wish to do, and all flames are like the best humans: they only seek to grow.

***

The kingdom didn't resurrect itself into a vibrant culture and energy without profound loss. They didn't worship suffering, but rather, they embraced it and used it. The culture encouraged it and its finely-tuned balance between delving into depression and feeling it deeply—loneliness and despair—in order to spur their stronger and stronger citizens onward. The farmers toiled and believed in whatever gods or god they wanted to believe in. The craftsmen took a renewed pride in their craft, smiling down at their creations while they wiped the sweat from their brow. Tapestries and pots and tables and chairs with ornate carvings became the standard of Idaza, the envy of the entire known world.

The city, through a renaissance of culture and freedom of thought and word, became the luscious green gem of the world. This gem's light shone throughout the sun's far-reaching peaks and the night's many valleys across the globe, attracting merchants and tourists from near and far.

But there was still so much to do.

How could a good story end in perfect harmony? It couldn't. No good story could.

***

"Storytime! Storytime!"

An old, mustachioed man chuckled. His fat gut wiggled as he laughed at the excitement of the group of grandchildren sitting with smiles. He remembered when he was that young. He looked out at the anxious children, all sitting with their eyes bright and their heads in their palms.

Wearing slippers and a suede robe, he slid his hand across the used cover of a single book.

"You kids want to hear the story?"

"Yes!"

"Yeah! Tell the story!"

The grandfather grumbled as he cleared his throat and opened to the first page of the book they all so loved. A familiar author wrote it. They knew his name, but not the man behind the pen, conjuring the stories that lay beloved in every home of the kingdom.

The grandfather started: "And then there were vast plains of many paths, wide woods of foul beasts, and roots to snag every step that the boy took…. The boy faced infinite paths and could walk anywhere. But in every trail he took, certain danger awaited him—vicious rippers of flesh and thieves and bushes of poison all waited to snag him and kill him for their gain. They wanted to eat him. To destroy the boy—all the forces that would hurt and steal souls from those that dared tread any place near it."

The children clapped. They all imagined their own pictures of what the old man read. They pictured some boy faced with loneliness and ferocious wolves, a harsh landscape meant only to hurt him. But they loved it. And why would they love such a story where a poor, vulnerable boy had the whole world to roam and everywhere dangerous, seeking only to torture and trip the boy? Why would the children rejoice in the demise of a character rather than their success and joy? Maybe there was joy in the snags and the fangs of the wolves along the perilous path? Maybe the children, deep down, loved that the boy was in danger. Maybe they wanted to be in danger themselves.

Maybe the children heard the story from their grandfather about a boy facing uncountable odds, vicious things that could make him sick and turn him green and kill him. They liked the fact that the boy could die. After clapping, the children flattened their ears and focused their eyes like zombies, like cold dolls, like focused statues toward all a common goal.

The children, wrapped up and in the story read to them, were bound by the story—all gathered and sitting attentively on the soft floor. They were grasped by the story of the boy alone in the woods facing certain danger, bodily harm, being clawed alive, eaten as his lungs still quenched for the last time, and his body shriveled after weeks of an empty, desperate stomach.

The children loved the picture of the lonely boy in danger because, deep down, they knew their lives meant nothing without peril. Endless life meant nothing. Bliss meant nothing without struggle and danger. They would (and could) never say that themselves, but they knew that stupid some boy in a silly story was relatable and lovable even simply because he threw himself against the odds despite the risk of death—painful death of flame and fang, itching and rotting... slowly, slowly, painfully.

These were the stories told after The Last Conjurer, survived in secret passing even after the Age of The Merchant. Oh, and just like every human that came before the children—the grandfather, even *his* ancestors—*they loved violence*. Yes, those young children *loved* violence. The young human animals salivated over the sweet sound of trickling blood and rejoiced over violence and the triumph over it. It was all evil and good and beautiful and disgusting, all dripping with purple rivers of death that tasted so lively. They understood. The children understood. They were taught to not be violent by parents who also loved it, watched it, and were it.

Purple blood reigned over their spirits like animals.

But the gray grandfather continued. "Each step for the boy was difficult. Harsh. Cold and wet. Every path proceeded a track that stood as a task too tall for the short boy that had yet to become a skilled man. He didn't know any better, and so he chose a trail that seemed to be the safest. But no trail was safe…." The only wisdom the boy gained was from wild savages of stripes.

Animals wanted his blood. The dirt thirsted for his body. And the children—the children loved to listen to how close he was to danger and death.

But they also listened to how close he could come to destruction without being destroyed. The grandchildren's hearts were swept up by how the boy could maybe—*maybe*—stay alive toward his goal of getting out of the woods and into a safer scenario.

But safety meant nothing if not for danger and death. "Death" was a dark demon that gripped the minds of the young. But the children didn't care while they listened to the story of some foreign boy. They sat quietly and enjoyed the violent story, not knowing that their lives only meant so much because of death, having no idea that they enjoyed the story of the boy *because* of danger. Their imaginations went wild with a tale of a lone soul that took the chances they would never take.

Their grandfather continued the story, and, as he spoke, the words dripped into the minds of the kids sitting quietly. They sat in wonder at what the character would do next, wanting different things for him and only wishing for his success because he risked death.

They loved hearing about the wolves howling, the demons that lurked in the dark, the monsters that made meals out of lost souls like the boy in the story.

The old gray man grumbled to clear his throat. "That's enough for tonight," he said. But the children all whined for more, disappointed that they wouldn't be able to hear what came next. The lonely boy in the story was a mirror to them, and they looked into the reflection without knowing it was them they loved or hated, their own lives they wanted to flee or escape.

"You'll find out soon, kids. I gotta go to bed." And as old men do, he grunted as he got up from his lazy chair and headed for his cushy bed.

The story was written, and the young listeners were hypnotized, but the rest of the tale remained untold for some time.

Without lack, there is nothing. Death may not be a gift, but it gives life its purpose. Those children already knew that in their hearts, every cell of their skin quaked with the love of fear for what came next. And what came next in the story would haunt them so pleasantly until the end of their living days.

Oh, stupid words! I can rewrite whatever came before you.

Chapter 4

A Kingdom Dies; One Man Cries

Coyote coughed. He sprinted past guards as they looked on in pity at the man that stunk of brown wine and purple dirt. Those guards knew what the boy would see. They were humans too, and they knew Coyote, and they knew what the dying king meant to him. They knew the story without saying a word, and they understood both the living Coyote and the dying king. But, as they were trained to do since birth, they stood straight and still, steady, always in the face of a threat. Their silver spears were sharp at the point.

"Where is he? Where is he? Where…."

"He's in his chambers, Coyote."

Rushing, striding, stumbling, heaving chest. He almost tripped again and hit his arm on a marble statue that would have crashed on the floor with a solid bang.

But he stopped as soon as he saw the door. He inhaled deeply, as deeply as he could, and closed his eyes. But when he saw only darkness in the pits of his lids, he grunted and charged toward the door, trying to bust open the thick wooden slab with his bony shoulder. It didn't budge. He gritted his teeth and slammed against the door again. The only thing that moved were his pained nerves bruising and bruising again. His breath got short again.

His shaking hand reached for the handle as an angry voice sounded from the other side: "Who goes there?" Cough. More coughing. Silence and coughing.

"It's Coyote. Let me in!" Coyote's eyes glared. Coyote's chest pounded. The memories of his painful past all reared their heads.

His faded family. His lost ties to love. It all stuck in his soul. He wanted to die right there with the king. Next to the king. His last tie to sanity—the king—was fraying and soon to break at a moment's notice.

But the wooden door opened with a creak.

He slipped inside and rushed to a giant bed where a gray man lay. His face lost its vibrant color from months away from the sun. Coyote pushed his hands on the king's bony shoulders.

"Agh," Oro whimpered. "Thahurts…."

Coyote's face darkened. He closed his eyes, trying to hide from Oro's sickly state and reach back to memories when he was a strong leader that stood on two feet, a man with a broad chest and a heart that loved people. Coyote, through closed eyes, pictured the king as a man who led with empathy and strength, hardened by loss, and motivated by hope. Coyote thought back to the time when Oro looked toward a scared boy as the last hope of a kingdom of people that all loved their lives and wanted to live happily with their families and friends.

But Coyote soon opened his eyes. Images of colorful times melted into a gray blur. He stretched his hand toward Oro's cheek and stroked it softly, slowly, with one finger, then two.

His eyes were so tired of crying. But the man's streaming tears and sobbing proved he couldn't run from his trauma. No pile of gold could bring Oro back.

Humans and beasts could be fought and killed. Pain could be overcome. But the Reaper of Death was unmatched and could not be defeated in the end. Coyote shivered.

He looked at the king's face. There was so much pain in his eyes. He seemed like some helpless animal then, not a mighty king. His face was pale, and his hands were bony and wrinkled. His pitch-black pupils were dark and deep. Coyote stared into them—the eyes of the king. He couldn't find a point in them to focus on. The king's eyes expanded as gaping black voids. Oro was no longer Oro, lying there with heavy breath. His eyebrows were just meshed bundles of fine gray hairs.

He was a helpless animal.

And as the life, the spirit, the memories, and the mark of the king left his forsaken body, so did the last of the boy. For as his past had died, he was no longer a boy but a man, still cloaked in a patchy brown hood. Although it was thin and coarse, he thought it would keep him warm through future storms.

"Oro…."

Coyote watched the flitting lids of the king's eyes shake to stay open. Those dying black pupils were still bold and strong. Death loomed, and its silent steps approached. The sunlit windows turned gray.

"Oro, Oro—stay with me."

He tried to cry, but the tears wouldn't come. He wanted to say so many things, but what was there to say? What words were worth it?

Oro lay in the bed unmoving; his chest stopped quivering. Quiet coughs echoed throughout palace halls, the still Inner Gardens, and even the streets of the sprawling city. All the world quieted to hear his one cough.

Coyote yelled at the doctors, guards, and priests to leave the room. "Go away! Get out! Now!" They all tucked their heads and filed out the door until all went still, and Coyote turned back toward the king's closing eyes.

"Oro! Uncle Oro! Please, please... stay with me."

One last groan escaped his gray lips.

"Stay with me…."

"I... *can't*, Coyote. No one can...."

And from tremendous black vats, great giant voids of pitch darkness, the king's pupils passed behind gray eyelids forever.

Coyote could never see enough death to know what it meant or what it was. As Oro's face and head stiffened, his eyes closed for the last time. Coyote didn't understand a dead or dying body. What was there to understand? Were bodies just flesh that moved until their time came to rot? That's what Coyote came to believe.

Coyote stared at the former king as he lay dying, dying, seizing up and going cold. Gray skin turned to white. Pale frost seemed to flake along his once-tanned flesh. Coyote felt in his bones the moment blood stopped pumping in the king's great body. His father figure died in his arms right then. But Coyote cried no tears. King Oro, once olive-red under the sun, laughing away a childhood of growing up as a forsaken son of a cold father, now lay as a white jumble of stiffening white flesh.

Coyote looked at the body—no longer a man, a king, a jolly father figure, a person. He just watched as the pile of pale flesh contracted, spit, gurgled, and groaned to a silent halt that sounded louder than any whistle could. Coyote watched as the man decayed and stiffened, dead,

dead as a leaf in late autumn. Oro was as dead as a chopped tree. His life was only a memory that flashed and then died as quickly as it came.

The young man in the hood watched. He couldn't take his eyes off the pile of cells and limbs. None of it held life any longer. And as King Oro's body lost its heart, brain, and skin, so did Coyote's mind leave him. His mind went away forever—it was the last possible thing to lose that he lost. Coyote just looked. His eyes were dry. He didn't blink. His eyes couldn't cry from years past. What would he cry for now? Another death? Another loss? Another piece of the puzzle of his life that broke? And what was death to him? What was death to a life that only knew loss? Nothing. It was all nothing. And what remained after someone's sense left them? After the body stiffened and went cold, there was nothing. Coyote believed there was nothing left.

No doctor, guard, or priest dared enter where the new king now stood.

They knew. All the people of the palace knew who commanded them now. The whole kingdom was now beholden to a different being, a different animated bag of flesh—this man was young and angry and bearded who wore one robe, brown and ragged with eyes colder than the moon. This new king—leader, emperor, sultan, or what have you—had no ideals. Coyote, unlike his father, had little art to give. Unlike King Oro, he lacked a big heart to care for others. Unlike the kings that came before him, Coyote had never taken a life in war and had never beheaded a savage. He'd never ordered anyone's death. He'd never been ruthless.

But he had known loss. He'd been orphaned and left behind. He'd been beaten. Unlike all the kings of the past, he knew the commons, he knew the slums, he knew homelessness and cold nights without hope or a mother to hold him.

And now, by law of the dead king's decree, this pitiful bearded boy was ruled over the largest city in the world. What the young man had to do with it, or what he wanted to do with it, was up to his sole will—his discretion held the precious lives of millions of beating hearts.

But to a man who met so much loss, sin, and so much anger, what were a few million lives?

A perfect government is only an idea—Coyote thought—as worthless as a prayer or a hope. Hope. There is no hope. There is no mercy. Coyote has never known that. In all he's seen and studied, hope was merely a word in a dictionary for fools. He had no use for hope. The last time he felt hope was when he reignited the city in a publication that reached the masses.

But the eyes of the man in the brown robe saw no hope, only death, only a dead man that no longer breathed the vapid air of life. He saw only a world that lived to die. Decay. But he grew up to love this decaying body as a second father in the absence of Mikalla, his father, who died before he could remember what he did that was so great and memorable for the kingdom. He watched the closest thing he had to a father die. Oro's body died slowly and then quickly; he convulsed in three snaps, and then frothed at the mouth. Coyote's heart and bones hardened as he watched his last tether to humanity die stiff and rotten in a common bed. He was thrust into a world that cared not for him once again. And once again.

And Coyote saw through the veil of the world as the frost-white body convulsed and stiffened. The body's mouth foamed. This is what he was given. He cared not for the throne Oro promised him. He didn't care about the kingdom he would inherit from his uncle. He cared about nothing. And because everything *and everyone* he cared about left him, he didn't know which emotion to turn to. He was angry at the dirt he stood on, at the gods, at the people that betrayed and beat him, and at the society that left him for dead. The Emperor thought about all those children that are cheated and stolen from—just like him. He was angry at life, at the price of a simple step in a world of victims and cuts and bruises.

He looked at the dead body for one more second. His whole body shook and fidgeted in a vitriol of violent and ripe hatred. He silently prayed for it all to stop.

Please, no more pain. Please, no more enemies. Please, whoever sent me or whoever made me... grant me peace... please. I beg. No more pain....

But as he jerked his eyes away from the body that was once a man, his prayers and hope halted. He damned the gods to Hell. He hated the gods. He hated the bed his uncle lay in. He hated the jungle full of death he was born into.

As the teeth and fangs of the young man stayed locked and tight, he let out a savage growl. He opened his mouth and his howl rang out through the palace and out the window, echoing in the Inner Gardens and throughout the city commons. It sent a shudder down every spine in the city that heard the screech.

It sounded like an abandoned dog howling in the lonely night without a pack or an owner to claim him. He sounded like Anger. His yell into the gray day was like a dog without a buddy—empty howls in the night. His howl sounded like rusty steel moaning from the mountains.

He screeched through white teeth. The white doves of death scattered and flew away. All that could be heard through the palace was screaming—a painful pitch. He yelled and howled into a night sky that didn't listen and just stood still. Coyote knew no one really cared about him—not anymore. Everyone that cared about him fled back. The dirt was his only birthright. He wanted to cut someone and see red. He was used to the smell of blood under the smear of a bleary night sky.

A dead body lay on top of a giant and lively city. But that dead body gave birth to a new leader. The new emperor wore a patchy brown cloak that stunk of death as he sat in the corner of the king's room, sobbing and guzzling wine until he puked. And then he guzzled some more until he fell asleep in a puddle of his own deep-green vomit. He sobbed in his sleep.

But those cold cinders of his soul never stopped smoking. There was always more to lose and more to scorch. His eyes burned bright despite the black night that came upon him.

He was only a small part of a cycle that would go on forever.

Human flesh was like the bark of a tree or the wings of a sparrow.

The awesome cycle of rebirth was only beginning to churn its discordant tone.

More burning. More fire. The flames were only *now* beginning to arise. Aha! Another life would spring anew. You'll see.

Chapter 5

A Jealous Priest

The king died, and the word spread quickly. The gray coughing body ceased to cough at some point. Death laughed.

Murmurs amongst the decorated noble people wondered who would pay them or who they'd have to take from. They shifted in the shadows, whispering in snake-like tones. One of them on that fateful day said this: "The crown seems to have been swiped by some orphan."

"No. That's impossible."

"I heard it was his nephew he appointed."

"Well, he's no king then, is he?"

Wealthy courtiers scattered all about the palace halls among whispers of the news. They all worked together and fought all the time in an eternal tempest; rich people with a lot to lose didn't fight with ferocity. The faceless nobility thought they held power, and they loved their own thoughts. They held their noses high and dressed in well-cut garments, well-pressed suits, and rich scarves that sparkled. Or maybe they didn't have power or much of anything other than influence. Either way, they all grasped for power by handshakes.

But the emperor still loomed over their heads; he was still the man that had to legitimize their precious power. Their shiny shoes. Their spotless robes and toned scarves of precious material. They personified the power of the state—all those nobles with their noses up. Their eyes were low and closed to the past, bent on their own future, as all they wanted was more. But who could blame them? Are you any better than these nobles? Those well-dressed people in the palace felt the pull of the power vacuum.

But power was a comical thing that humans held and God laughed at.

***

Lupus was the High Priest of Idaza, who walked straight with his head high and his eyes always shifting to potential threats. He was Coyote's uncle, his mother's last living brother. The religious leader stood still amidst the chaos of courtiers rushing around. They paced quickly with shifting eyes. He silently laughed as they rushed by, going quickly but carefully enough to not scuff their leather shoes. He was Jani's brother, cousin of the late King Oro, and one of the last blood relatives of The True King, the royal bloodline of Menizak The Great, founder of the Kingdom of Idaza.

Lupus looked on with silent eyes as all his enemies lay dead at his feet. He had only one last obstacle to his rightful throne: Coyote, the petulant bearded boy with no plan.

His blood boiled with even the slightest thought of the big old, spoiled boy given the world without ever having to take anything for himself. Or so he thought. To

Lupus, Coyote was a mess of a man who quaked at every tiny shake of the earth.

Lupus, the high priest, the self-righteous heir to the souls of the people below him, thought to himself as the courtiers all walked around trying to look busy and important: *this little brown smudge on humanity has no right to anything—his father was a great man who married into royalty. But I knew my sister before our cousin had her killed; she didn't care for Mikalla. She cared about what she could get from him. She may have been dim-witted, but she was smart enough to marry The Conjurer, who was also a close friend of the king. But their offspring, Jani's only child—that ragged, hairy, unkempt kid. He's an abomination. He did do one good thing in his pathetic life: oppose Kitan's plans. Kitan's visions of the future of Idaza would completely undermine my position, and I thank Coyote and his Uncle Oro for getting rid of that sniveling snake. But this little man that sulks in brown robes has to go.*

Lupus put his hand to his chin as he leaned against a giant pillar in the middle of the palace. The shadow of a statue darkened the priest's face. *I stand among idiots and losers. All my enemies have fallen. All that have opposed me over the decades—Oro, his father, Oro's broad brother, Kitan, Jani, Yolia, Mikalla, my petulant brother Gobi, the Men in Masks, all the rest of my siblings, and the last three generals of the army—are all dead. They all lie stiff and gray in the ground. And yet I live. And yet, by the grace of the gods, I stand tall and strong. Every enemy of mine is gone. I thank the gods for that. The rest that surround me are just fat, ignoble people that only care about worthless gold coins and big houses. All my adversaries are dead. They have no say in the present or the future.*

I shall utter the final word.

Lupus shivered in the shadows and bit his lip.

Except one. One last remnant of the past remains above the ground. One of my enemies stays breathing, albeit pathetically. Coyote. Son of The Last Conjurer and my royal-blooded sister. He is the child of the kingdom itself. My last obstacle to power now sits on a rickety throne, and now I can strike. I have remained motionless for too long. I needed Oro while he lived. Then I needed him to die.

But now I need only one more body to fall. He will be killed at the top and rest forever in the dirt.

A Letter From The Conjurer

Chapter 6

The Bearded Child With Power

As the new Emperor of Idaza, Coyote vacated the palace in favor of staying in his childhood house, which he finally got to reclaim after years of homeless wandering. It was as if, instead of inheriting the kingdom, he inherited the only thing he could have without the king having died. It was all a web of legal and illegal dealings, paradoxes reaching far in between alleys of dark shades and sharp edges.

He felt safe in his home, empty, except for a single trusted servant who he believed would never sell him to the wolves.

But the supposed 'son of a great man' was still encased in quivering flesh that wanted to rule over an environment that moved without him and cared little for his well-being. Coyote let his advisers and royal courtiers live and play in the royal palace where King Oro used to reside. Soon after Oro died, it became more of a giant resort of debauchery and recreation instead of work. Coyote could have held the royal courtiers accountable. But his mind seemed screwed into an eternal cyclone, jumbled and washed away into an endless drain. He didn't think for one second about the advisers and wealthy noble people except for keeping them satisfied and fat. He still lay in his childhood bed, untouched from where he left it all those years ago. Above his desk, the glow of the morning sun illuminated a giant mural of a great man enchanting a whole kingdom with his stories and words.

If there is such a thing as the true essence of a person, what would that pearl constitute? How would you describe the core of a person? Is it their soul? Is it their heart? Is it their mind? Is it their gut?

Well, Coyote's whole soul shunned his "royal" court and his kingdom as he transitioned swiftly into the role of Emperor of Idaza per Oro's dying decree. Almost all of the noble people, courtiers, and royal extended family didn't care who sat on the throne, but rather just riches and luxury and big banquets they could enjoy. They didn't care that Coyote now sat on the throne. In fact, they preferred an indifferent emperor who didn't care what they did. That's why those thoughtless nobles wanted power in the first place: to satisfy their carnal pleasures: drink, sex, fatty food, sunlight, and laughing at parties until dawn shone through the giant palatial windows.

But what of Coyote—the paralyzed emperor? He never stopped grieving ever since he was a simple boy.

What of Lupus—the ambitious high priest? Coyote knew little about Lupus, only that he was his uncle, the High Priest of Idaza.

What would come of the kingdom that had yet to hear about the passing of their king? The people were once again left in the dark until further notice.

But there were a couple other players in this grievous game. There were others that abided the darkness, biding their time to take a bite of what they wanted. And desire drove these people.

But peace is a lie. It would always be a lie so long as a good story is told. A good story cannot be peaceful. What does that say about you?

Chapter 7

New Blood

As soon as he heard the news of the fallen king, Tozl lurked around the royal palace, waiting for his right time to enter. A lifetime bureaucrat hidden in shadows who sparkled in the brightest of shade. But he wanted more respect—one big career fast-track he was happy to shake, nod, and smile through, so long as it sucked him closer to the vortex of power at the center of Idaza. Now, this smelly boy was the center of a once-proud government, and he had to pay his respects and bow down as he was so used to. He squinted at the great mass of brick and marble and gold. His body tensed up. But he paid no attention to his body, only his surroundings and the careful tides of power as they portrayed gold and satin-silk—he had a keen nose for luxury. He just wanted to stay in the good graces of power ever since his old master died. He strode toward the home of the center of power, of Idaza, of his known world.

He wore a purple-and-gold silk dress and spotless slippers that seemed to float as he sauntered about his mansion. For the first time in his life, he had a plan he devised all on his own. He dismissed his servant-spy away from him and his house as he made his way down the stairs. He mastered the art of looking effortless, even if there was no one to look his way.

But soon people would look. Soon, people would appreciate him. And why did he want so many to take in his bright dresses and straight smile? That didn't matter to him. His mind was too cramped with the will of others.

He felt a sense of freedom for the first time in forever. And he was about to throw all of that freedom away.

He had a thought pass through his head as he stepped down the stairs toward a different destiny. His essence exuded refinement and luxury. With his master now dead, he had all the freedom and wealth he ever wanted; it was all he worked for his whole life. He'd always been an agent, a sort of servant of the state without any real agency—a silk-clad servant smiling his way to the center of the vortex. But as he'd finally made his way to his goal—that long-sought center of the vortex—he still wanted more. He wanted to see more, do more, and bow to greater powers so long as he could afford foreign shoes and the shiniest things gold coins could buy. He had no message to deliver, but he was damn good at delivering messages.

He finally floated out his front door onto a path of more work and even more wealth. But freedom? Well, his mind was never wired for freedom. He liked being handcuffed so long as the chains were solid gold. Tozl only knew the cost of his clothing and not the price of his freedom.

He stepped into the sun, a bright and open day where he could have done anything he wanted. He may have been adorned in silk and bright satin, but all he desired to wear were the shackles of a greater man.

***

Coyote awoke in broad daylight next to a jumble of empty wine bottles. His ringing ears peered toward a slight knock at the door and a yell from his lone servant.

"Master! Master Coyote… you have a visitor." His servant's words sounded like a giant jumble in his ringing ears, splitting his vision in two.

"Who…. What?"

The voice echoed closer to his chambers. It was a quiet whisper compared to the yelling before. "You have a visitor, Coyote. He claims his name is Tozl. He claims he is the emperor's diplomat... and that he's at your service."

Coyote groaned. His head throbbed. His gut felt green, and his raspy throat felt red. "Tellimtowait."

"What was that, Master?"

"I said, 'tell him to wait!'" It hurt his head to yell so loud.

Coyote heard mumblings from down the stairs in the grand entryway.

He arose in his dirty robe. It stank of wine and bad breath and the odor of someone who has quit on life. To others, the brown ratty robe may have been looked at as a sign of defiance or humility. But Coyote just wore it because his blood ran cold from many bitter nights against the dark desert. It was the only trusted companion he had always, his only consistent piece in a life that changed constantly. His smelly brown cloak could be either a lion's mane or the dirty pelt of a wolverine. Either way, it had a vicious scent that repelled others. But the new emperor didn't care. What was a fine linen other than a fading feeling? What was cleanliness if not to impress others? Coyote cared about none of this, and, eventually, he rambled down the steps with sore legs and a green gurgling stomach. Maybe he gained weight. Maybe he lost weight. He never looked in the mirror long enough to consider what he looked like.

He met the last step of his giant staircase of his family home. He was hopelessly out of shape. His short lungs drew shallow breaths. He heaved short breaths as he trudged down the steps, too traumatized to care who was there. His dim mind fogged as he wished it were the Lord Mictlan, the very God that could put him to death and end the life he was so scared to live any longer.

But his guest was not a god that greeted him at the door. Rather, it was a mere man that stood at average height in a bright dress. He had no features about him that stood tall, handsome, or large. This human had no special qualities besides pristine slippers and a clean silk robe. Much to the emperor's chagrin, it was not the God of Death that stood in his entryway to take him to an easier place. Instead, it was Tozl, the hungry leech that only craved the blood of others. He watched Tozl with the eyes of a fox. Coyote at that moment cared not for power. The steps down his childhood home seemed foreign to him as he looked at the smiling nobleman. He cared about nothing and welcomed the man with a simple greeting.

Tozl beamed and seemed to glow with a bright smile. His teeth were ivory white. He kneeled in front of his emperor, bowing his head to the marble floor of the mansion. Tozl may not have known much, but he had a knack for sensing power. He knew he was in the midst of the greatest power in the world.

"Your Majesty, it is a privilege and a blessing to be in your midst."

Coyote stood still. "Rise."

Tozl stood straight back up. "My name is Tozl, and I serve as your diplomat to foreign lands. I served your... *ahem*—I served King Oro before you. My job is to be your right hand to extend to foreign nations as you see fit. My only mission is to serve you. I have a long history of traveling, and I specialize in communications between leaders and kings of the like."

The emperor's sad eyes met the diplomat. For some reason, this man's bright smile and gleaming robe made Coyote's mood turn dreary.

"Your Majesty, I only wish to serve your will. I came to let you know that I am your tool."

Coyote bit his jaw. "You are a tool, and I don't need anything fixed. All will turn to its natural order."

"Your Majesty..."

"Call me 'Coyote.' That's the name my parents gave me. My parents gave me this house, too. Oro gave me this kingdom. I was given everything. My past lovers gave me scars. My past stories gave me freedom. My experiences give me pain. If you seek only to serve, then be still."

"And when you say to be still, what do you mean?"

"I mean to silence your speech, quiet your mind, and stop your legs. Let all things be given to you. That's all I have learned. In a way—as some emperor—I'm supposed to serve you. But the more you serve, the more you are given things that you learn to receive, especially if you have to walk through flames in order to learn that lesson."

Tozl shook in his velvet slippers. He shivered at the great man's words. He had no question; this was a great man he beheld. But how could he be so much better wearing only rags? This young man didn't seem to clean himself or look like anything to anyone. He was only a body, a vessel, a cup to be filled. He was nothing but a vehicle for the stars and the wicked gods.

But how? Tozl wondered how this man achieved so much in a shorter time than he did.

But Tozl hung on his last tether; he was a salesman at heart. A true salesman either sold or died, and Tozl had yet to die.

"How can I be still if life's only constant is change?"

These words then threw Coyote aback. Coyote's gray-sad mood turned to an angry thunderstorm that shook the marble floor they both stood on. "I told you what I've been given. If you refuse to be still and fall to your flesh, then *suffer*." The ragged emperor marched toward the diplomat until they met face-to-face. Tozl smelled the emperor's rancid wine breath. "Suffer, then. Go and grind your bones to dust and then pay the true price of success, and then come back to me. That would be the only worthy man to serve me! Go scratch and steal and beg for your future meal, and then come to me! That's the only journey that moves me and anyone else worth living…. Be gone. Go and learn, think, or just sit and drink or drug yourself until you sleep. I don't care about a servant—I'm a servant, too. I don't care about your ambition—I'm ambitious, too. *Go. Now*."

Tozl looked away from the man, even if he was younger. He seemed to have something in his chest that rang through the deserts of the world with a whisper. Tozl bowed deeply to a knee and then left without a word. It would not be the last time he saw the emperor, and it wouldn't be the last time he felt something he never felt before.

It wouldn't be the last time Tozl did something he never did before: leave without a word. He didn't know what to do, so he turned and left. Maybe that was the point. He couldn't be harmed if he never harmed anyone else, right?

He scuttled back to his house, dodging the dew from the wet grass so it didn't

***

Coyote wanted to talk, to speak, to have a careful ear for his words. But he dismissed his servant so he could be alone. He sent his servant to his quarters and stood in the empty entrance of the house.

He stood cold. He stood staring at the marble. That man in fine linens seemed like nothing, only a gasp of air in the universe to an emperor that could decide anything. But as he was human, and as he stood as a leader over many humans, the man thought he'd go be among other humans. He didn't want to step out of his house, and yet his feet moved and his body followed. The emperor never desired to leave, but desire was a stupid, silly thing.

He left to chase the soul of the kingdom through his front door.

He left on weary feet to feel again despite the darkness of his mind. He gritted his teeth to feel the light no matter how much the sun may hurt his head, no matter how much the chattering of the nobility would give him a groan.

Anger was the most powerful tool in a world fueled by the fire and the spear. They would all see soon.

Chapter 8

Oro's Awakening

There was so much not around, so much missing in this new place where Oro now found himself. He thought he died as an old gray corpse, and yet he stood there as a sun-kissed man with big white teeth smiling. He looked down at his sandals; his nails were long and his feet were tanned.

Heavenly sunshine poured through tall and bright windows in a big room surrounding the lone man. His skin was leathery, and he had a great gut from years of laughter and wine—sad eyes and a wide brow. Fine leather sandals supported his burly frame. He was a broad man who smiled to keep from crying.

He marveled like a child in wonder at the giant house with sky-tall ceilings and bright, sunlit windows. The chandelier glistened with crystals hanging high above his head.

He stomped through the entryway into the vast white living room. The man cleared his throat, and it echoed throughout the vast halls of the mansion. He sat down and tried to relax his back, stomach, shoulders, and mind, wondering what was going on. He closed his eyes and saw only black. But somewhere in his dreams were melting murals that snatched his mind. They were pictures of shadows shifting around a reddened background like a cave that never ended. He refused to see and think further into these visions as his eyes popped open and he took in a deep breath.

His lungs got heavy, and he slouched over, looking at the ground that seemed to swirl all around him. His feet got heavy and his body tensed again; muscles tightened as he stopped breathing altogether, biting his cheek and shivering.

Oro was never considered a wise man, but the opinions of others never had an impact on one's grasp of nature.

He stayed looking at the marble floor turn and twist beneath him. He whispered to himself, *"I'm here for a reason."*

As his head bobbed in the sea of vertigo, purple rushes in the green vortex of nausea, he finally looked up, hoping his aches and pains went away—if only for a moment.

But when he looked, all he saw was a figure cloaked in gray, with a gray beard and cold gray eyes that sat atop a mountain of a man.

It was his father. The King of Idaza—the last true king of the great Menizak Dynasty. His name was Menizak, just like his father and his father before him. Oro may have been his son, but he shared not the name of the only one he looked up to. Instead, that sacred Menizak name was reserved for someone else—Oro's late older brother.

"Father…."

"Oro."

"What are you doing here?"

"The value of a man is not where he is, but who he is. Why I'm here has no bearing on who I am, and I am Menizak The Third. I am the king of kings."

His son's husky, tanned body shriveled like a scared child.

And then Oro's memories came flooding back. He saw, painfully, all the strife he caused throughout his storied life. He watched the betrayal he faced in his mind's eye like a nightmare. But his nightmare was his life. The cold regret of letting his friend die. The burning vengeance he felt against all who did it—all the snakes he allowed to slither in *his* royal palace. He thought of all the romance he lost out on. He would love to say that he just didn't care enough. But the fact was, he was a great, big coward. He thought about all the crags and roots that tripped him on the path to becoming a full-grown king. He thought about his helplessness to drink. He thought about all the countless nights

But even after death, he didn't quite know why and how it all happened. It just seemed like in the prime of his aging life, he rampaged against enemies. But later on, after a life of laying down and enjoying the fruits of a royal boy eating and drinking everything around him, he stood up and acted. Oro—after the ghosts of a life of treachery and pity bled from his memory—stood on his own two feet, gritting his teeth, and finally taking command.

"You taught me a lot of things, Dad. Once my older brother died—"

"Don't speak of your older brother again! Menizak carried the name of the greatest legacy in the world!" His father exploded with fury that angered his face and clenched his hands. He huffed through a tight jaw. He looked like he wanted to smash something, but there were only cushy couches that sat in the empty room. Oro's father didn't sit down. His mouth twisted into slow disgust looking at his grown pudgy son. The former mighty king looked down on his second son with venomous angry eyes, noticing tanned skin from the sun and smile marks and wrinkles from fun parties with flowing wine. "Your brother was a true warrior! He fought through pain and unleashed the terror of the gods on our many enemies. But you... you haven't felt and fought the pain, the divine tests the gods chose for us. You refused that test."

He shook his head and stood great and gray, like an armored statue ready for war.

But there were no warriors to fight. There were no enemy soldiers or areas to conquer—not even a battlefield where he could draw plans and command troops. He had no one to fight in the vast white room. He only had his second-born son who sat before him—not a warrior in body nor spirit. Oro was not the son he asked for and never the successor he wanted.

But Oro lived a full life after his father died. He became king and lived out trials of tough decisions, slowly losing everything in a hellish centrifuge of a life that limped onward, persisting passed the grip of trauma, the guilt of a man who put all imaginary pain on his own shoulders—on his own conscience—as he continued to walk through a path he never felt he was meant for. Caught. Trapped. Encaged at the top of the kingdom, weighed down by the heavy crown and the gold of the goblets he so often drank from.

But the prodigal son sat with no wine.

The broad gray king stood stolid with no sword.

They each only had themselves; they only had each other in a world far off but not unlike our own.

"Father, you have caused me a lot of pain—"

"You've never felt a lick of pain in your life, son! You've never even been scratched by a cat, nonetheless, wounded by a sword! And now," Menizak's face darkened in anguish. His memory paths traced back to terrible times of loss, leading the way for an uncertain future he hated. "Now, you sit here soft and worn from a wasted life. That life was a gift, and you've *squandered it*. Our kingdom has been overrun with thugs and bandits, raiding the coffers my father fought so hard to keep."

"But who gave me this life?"

"What do you mean? The gods gave you life. I gave you everything else."

"No." Oro stood up. "No. *You* gave me life. *You* brought me into the world as your second addition to a family *you* led. But you treated me like a... like a tool."

Through spit and bared teeth, the gray king stepped closer to Oro, doing what he'd always done to an opponent—intimidate them. Intimidation was the Menizak way. Intimidation and screeching battle cries of war founded the nation that the broad gray man ruled over for so many decades.

But Oro was no longer intimidated—not by his father or his past on an earth that passed by him. Not intimidated by his duties. He no longer scared himself. He felt for the first time like he could look into his own reflection and smile from within.

"You were a prince, Oro, and I treated you as such. You were the *second prince*, and so I gave you all I could after...." His father's face saddened. He couldn't quite finish his sentence.

"After my brother died."

"After your brother died, I taught you the only way *you* could rule! You were never a warrior. You weren't *made* to *fight.* You were made to—"

"To rule. And ruling, Father, does not always require fighting."

The men stared at each other.

Oro stopped shivering. His body didn't quiver as he faced his life's largest shadow. He looked at his father and even heard mocking whispers of his late older brother—his *better*, older brother.

"Life is a fight, Oro. I told you all about the snakes that would inevitably surround your feet. I warned you of the thorns. I taught you about this world and how everything in it wants to eat you or cut you to pieces. I taught you how to *rule* as well. I taught you how to keep an iron grip on power. I taught you how to be a good king!"

"You did teach me important lessons through your words. But I always felt like you showed something different—like I could never amount to my brother. I was always the second option."

"And you were my second born! I was the king. He was my *first* successor. What don't you get about that? Obviously, you were my second option. Is that not obvious, Oro? Why was that never apparent to you? Were you not smart enough to see the natural flow of the kingdom and our lineage? You were the *Second* Prince of Idaza. THE *SECOND* PRINCE!" His father slammed his fist against the table, shattering the glass all over the floor. The shards glowed like crystals in the beam of the light.

Oro kept his voice soft. He did his best not to shiver and, instead, sat still facing his red-faced father.

"I was the Second Prince, yes. I was also your second son. *Your* son." Oro looked up and locked eyes with his father. "Dad, I came from you. You raised me differently from my brother, but that's fine. I don't mind being treated differently—we were different people. But I was treated *less than*. My whole life, I felt like an ant, an afterthought. That's something that... hurt." Oro's eyes welled and reddened with soft tears. "It hurt me a lot... my whole life. I carried that hurt my whole life."

Menizak took a deep breath and seemed to calm down some. "But you knew I loved you, Oro. I always told you that." The man paced the floor looking with empty eyes, searching for answers for his son. "As a father, not just as a king, I loved you."

Menizak felt the warmth of his grown son's tears trickle through his veins. After losing his life and handing over his kingdom, what else did he have besides the legacy he looked at then?

Not the second prince—his second son.

Oro mumbled to respond to his father.

"What was that?"

Oro mumbled again louder, moving his lips a little stronger, putting his full stomach into his words for his father. He hoped his voice would be heard. He hoped his words would be received. But only time would tell. He had to, for once in his life, act on his instincts.

Chapter 9

The Holy Wolf Promises The World

Metzli wore a black and clean silk suit as she strutted around the royal palace. She was not a royal, not of noble birth, and yet she was there, right there in the middle of it all, striding tall among the noble men around the endless palace walls. She held strong arms with a steely stride around the luxurious epicenter of the kingdom. She walked past marble busts of important statesmen she studied in school.

The woman wore strongly woven satin and a steely look on her face—once a young girl who only wished to take a look inside the gleaming walls of the palace as an outsider. The young girl who traded bread for cheap coins always focused on gems, not copper. For so long, she wanted the jewels and all the pretty things that shined that she could never have as a mere girl from the city commons, selling bread and avocados for meager pay to feed her family.

But after years of mining the many diamonds from the men, surfing the silk sheets of the secretaries, and spilling the kingdom's gold into her gilded hands, she grew tired of a life of leisure. Sighing every morning and every night alone, her ambitions slowly shifted. Slowly, her mind cradled even grander visions of more—wider spaces and oceans of green emeralds glistening off the setting sun with a cup of deep burgundy.

It could all be so simple, she thought. She thought that all her life, meanwhile complex schemes dominated her mind all the time.

She started to see the diamonds differently after she clutched them in her hand. The gems lost their luster, and the gold lost its gleam once it fell into her hand. Her point of view changed—from just another yelling voice in the streets selling bread to a silk-clad noblewoman bedazzled in jewels and gems in major mansions atop the scenic world.

After getting what she wanted after all those years of selling simple bread, she thought she would've been happy. No, quite the contrary—the hole in her soul grew to a gaping gash that could not be satisfied by parties, handsome bodies, diamond rings, or silk slippers. There was nothing that made her happy. And now she was left in the middle of a non-stop storm of debauchery and wildness as courtiers and nobles rushed around the palace drunkenly throughout the endless days and nights. They all had the money, of course, to have the wine soaked up from the floor, the broken glass swept away, and the walls cleaned spotless once more—all this just to party another night, for just one more rush, one more chance to drink and undress, spill more wine, and break more glass with blank smiles and wicked laughs that haunted the palace's halls late into every morning.

The look on Metzli's determined face had a cruel touch to it—not an ounce of wine did she have that day. Nobody she touched, no money she spent. She spoke with no one but instead looked on from a private room of the palace that she claimed as her own after some time. Noble people would come in and out, but eventually, they all saw that room as hers and only hers, with no one having the authority (or care) to kick her out. To the mess of the noble people playing constantly, she was just a pretty fixture that got tired of partying as she grew from girl to woman.

She looked down in disgust at the complacency of the people who were supposed to lead the kingdom, guide the people, and control the policies of the emperor.

The Emperor.... Where is he? I wonder how he is. She thought about the man from years ago, long before he was ever in power, and before she ever had a taste for gold and rich wine. Way back then, if only for a few fleeting moments, they seemed to connect in a way she had never connected with anyone before. But that spark with Coyote seemed now to be a gray cinder in the sand.

Metzli thought about his boyish face—his sad eyes that seemed to hold wisdom beyond his young years. She would never forget that face, that time, that boy.

And then she jumped as she heard a knock on her door.

"Yes? Who is it?"

A strong voice echoed through the thick wooden door. "This is Lupus, the High Priest of Idaza. I was wondering if I could come in and talk."

Metzli twisted her face and crept toward the door. "What would you like to talk about?" Her shoulders tightened into her torso, searching for a reason as to why a man with so much to do would want to talk to her, of all people. Was she being watched? Did they find out she was not born of noble blood? Is this her punishment for infiltrating the Inner Gardens from the common class?

Metzli's mind spun and wound in a million circles. *What do I do? I surely can't get out of this…. Who would've investigated me?*

"I have a proposition you may like, Metzli."

The young woman shivered, wondering how the High Priest of Idaza knew her name.

"Ummm…."

"Metzli, I know you have more ambitions than the rest of these *creatures*. My prayer and sacrifice to the gods has given me insight into you. They have led me to you…. I just want to speak for a moment."

"Are you with anyone?"

"I come alone. I act completely by myself."

"What did the gods say about me?"

"I look forward to telling you if you'd be so kind as to let me in."

Metzli shivered. But, possibly, on the other side of that great wooden door lay a horizon for the new possibilities she'd been looking for. Maybe, by answering Lupus' call, she'd be opening another door, a new gateway to the things that could grant her what she lacked in her boring life. Her slender hand trembled as she reached for the lock.

Lupus appeared in a simple, straight white robe that clashed with her stark black suit. He smiled softly and greeted her with a gentle voice. "May I come in?"

***

They sat on the patio, overlooking the royal courtyard. Nobles sauntered around and littered scraps as servants scrambled to pick up after their mess. The hum of the palace's people sounded like one giant beehive. Since the steady buzz echoed all over the halls, their conversation could be had in secret.

Metzli bowed her head and closed her eyes. This was the first time she had knelt for any man, yet there she was, nearly kissing the ground out of respect for the High Priest. The people may not have believed in the gods, but the kingdom did. The kingdom was run by the High Priest's prayers behind closed doors in dark rooms. So much of what the man did was a mystery, rarely ever seen, nonetheless spoken to. "What were you seeking in your prayers, Your Holiness?"

"Please, just call me 'Lupus.' That's my name."

"Okay."

"Well, Metzli, I sought *direction* as I always do. From the *Gods*...." He coughed with dead eyes up to the pale-stained ceiling. "*I* asked for guidance from the gods. Me and them have a... special relationship." The High Priest raised his eyebrows, his tone, and his hands, staring straight into the woman's eyes. "You know, humans are merely servants to the gods, and we are lost without their ever-watchful eyes." He shook his head slowly. "I seek guidance from their many wisdoms as the kingdom's tether to the plane of the unknown." Then, the man leaned in to face her closer. "Direction is all I can really pray for—you don't *really* think that as humans, we have any power without the masters of the spiritual plane, do you?"

Metzli shook her head. "Oh, of course not! We have nothing—we, we *are* nothing—without the gods."

Lupus sat back in his chair and softened his voice. "Good."

"What direction did they give you? You said they led you to *me*? Why me? What did they say? What… did they want?"

Lupus looked up at the vaulted ceiling as if he were staring at the gods themselves. They seemed to look back into his eyes and, in turn, poured wisdom and truth into his words. "Metzli, they graciously gave me, after much thought and prayer, the image of you. Your aura defines what they—not *I*—have been looking for. They want you, Metzli, to rise and command. They told me many things…." Lupus stared off into the distance. His body— the motions of his hands and lips—seemed to put her in some sort of daze, where she thought she could see the very will of the gods herself. "But not through words. No. *No*. They told me through visions what would come of you—a young girl like you from the commons, once a humble worker in the city just trying to provide for her family—"

"Wait! How'd you kno—how'd you think of that? What made them say that I was once a commoner? What do you know about me?"

"Silence... and stillness, Metzli. I didn't think of any of this. I didn't picture any of this. It was only by the will of our gracious gods who give to us every day that I was granted these visions of both your past and your future."

Metzli squirmed in her chair. She tried to hide her whole body, shivering under her smooth back suit. She quaked at the priest's words. He seemed more like some freak prophet than a holy man. *And what does he want*? She thought to herself. But she knew her status was solid among a vast pool of lazy nobles. She understood that she could take what she wanted—that is, within reason and without angering anybody else. She never tried to upset others if she could avoid it. She remembered how her parents fought when she was a child.

She leaned her head in. "What did the gods tell you I'd become?"

Lupus knew right then, by reading her body like a book, that her words spilled right into his palm, only for his control. He already had control of her mind and, with it, her *will*."

"With my help, the gods have a grand plan for you that you can... *achieve*."

"And what is that?"

"Power. More power. A divine purpose that will make you an enormously powerful being above the kingdom."

Metzli smirked. The woman uncrossed her legs and looked away from the man with full lips exposed like fresh spring petals, laughing and smiling. *He will finally deliver me to my destination. This man can finally give me all I've dreamt about and escape this stupid palace. Hopefully, I won't have to hurt anyone. And if I do, I pray to the gods I don't believe in that I stay safe.*

Lupus held a stoic face, only seeing the back of the woman's head as she looked away. He needed to get inside that mind. He wanted her thoughts, not her heart. *I must know! What hidden ghosts lurk behind her mind I can prey on?*

But the woman turned away from the man. Her bright face was hidden by her long hair. And she smiled by herself, gaining another step on her ladder. She just wanted to climb up the social ladder in pretty shoes, loyal only to her image.

Chapter 10

Be Delivered From Pain

Jani eyed the silver dagger. Her teeth gnashed under her lips, cutting her cheeks and slicing her tongue. Her white fangs clanged and scraped. Her family's dagger shone by shadow like chrome, etched by the finest hands in the kingdom long ago, made with the care of an artisan's focus. The creation was as beautiful as it was deathly sharp. It looked like it could sprint or kill on its own, as if it had its own life somewhere buried underneath its decorative patterns and fine silver decorations. But under all of it, there was a will to kill, a desire to destroy.

A person's appearance describes a vital part of who they were, and so the vital parts of Jani were slender and smooth-skinned, the color of light java, streaking eyes that could cut into stone with a stare, and big and beautiful lips. She was a goddess that graced the earth with her beauty. She carried herself, standing tall and strong above the millions of commoners below her feet.

Her eyes, a meld of sharp green and gray and brown, stayed fixed, staring at the dagger on the table. She looked at the weapon; Mikalla looked at her like a helpless dog that only wanted affection from his owner. He looked at her as an infant would look up to its mother. A mortal to a god. A servant to a queen. And who was she to hold such power over a great man's heart? Well, there was a lot more within the mind that trickled out of mere labels and fine lines. The heart is a mesh of a web of entangled mass, stuck in a place that only pain could form. Only pain could give the human heart its impossible shape—a pain that no other animal could know. Mikalla's heart was shaped around Jani. It was forged by her hammer. It still beat for her.

Jani pushed Mikalla away and walked towards the dagger. The room was like a giant white cavern. Her footsteps were slow and small, echoing on the marble, bouncing off the walls and ringing in Mikalla's ears. She continued to make her way towards that silver piece.

Mikalla choked up a bit. He didn't know what would come on the other side of death. He didn't really understand death itself. He thought he died, but now he was kind of alive.

As he watched his beloved wife walk to the knife to kill him, he thought of his son. How nice, how heavenly, how at ease he'd feel if he were here in his arms. He pictured his young child as memories in his head flooded in. Mikalla watched his boy grow up, take his first steps, say his first words, and become a little person of his own. Coyote. Coyote was the boy's name. But Mikalla never got to see him as a man. The treachery and brutality of the world never allowed for Mikalla to be there for when Coyote grew up. The black death of regret seeped its tendrils into Mikalla's body as he thought about his son. *His son*—his only child. Coyote was the only boy, the only person, the only *idea* that a storyteller such as himself could never put into words the exact right way. There was no way to tell how Mikalla felt about Coyote. His son. That was his life. His next chapter was his son. No matter how fast the world spun or how hot the earth burned, that boy Coyote meant more to him than his own life. He was ready to be cut, slashed, and sliced. But the dark eyes of his boy—the son he held and kissed so long ago that laughed as he got tickled—he didn't know where those dark eyes may have gone. He left him a note long ago, but that was in a time of duress. The Last Conjurer knew nothing of his son's whereabouts, his life, his loves, his passions, his joys and pains, or even if he was still alive. But alive was a stupid word. As long as Mikalla knew that his son lacked his father, he knew he would live forever. He wanted him to be the best. He wanted so many things from Coyote, but also, paradoxically, to be his own person. It was the psychic struggle of every parent that had a vision for their children, but, also, at the end of the life of a man, his child reigned his mind; the little boy in his mind reigned over his mind like a king or the most violent cyclone. Thoughts of Coyote surged through the father's veins as his wife approached the weapon that would slit his vital veins in his neck. He awaited his death from someone he loved more than the moon. He thought about his son, his sun as the star that kept him warm, the sun that gave his life purpose.

Ohh! It all sliced his neck before a knife ever touched his skin. The thought of his lost and forgotten son hurt his veins more than any skin or spear ever could. He lost his son. He died before he could see his son grow up and see joy. He wondered what Coyote was up to now. He broke down to tears at the thought of Coyote being dead or hurt or scared or anything like that.

Mikalla, the powerful Conjurer of a thriving kingdom so in tune with what he had to say—the ruler of the hearts and minds of the entire known world—cried and cried. He sobbed for his son.

Mikalla cried for Coyote, his lone child he never got to watch grow up.

He loved his wife with his whole existence—this untouchable girl he met decades back in school he could never have. But his son. His son was hopefully some lost soul who could still fend for himself on his own two feet. They both could only pray he was healthy. But they didn't think he could possibly be well if he were still alive in the kingdom they left for him—one full of snakes with fangs and crawling creatures that lurked in the night, waiting to sink their venom with a bite.

Guilt was a bigger killer than the spear.

Coyote, his young son with those big boyish eyes, was Mikalla's joy, but also the greatest source of his pain as Jani grabbed at her dagger. He thought about that boy. He pondered the knife. And when she grasped for that dagger, she felt like she grasped for that power she always wanted. She had never killed but always wanted to. Maybe. But her husband? Would she really kill the person who seemed to love her most? Her grip struck a tiny chord that strummed sad memories of a small girl with no dreams of anything much. It felt like she fell into a life with a child and a family and a powerful position in the government that was never her own, yet she owned it all the same. *The portrait of a strong and beautiful woman dissatisfied.*

And did she ever ask to be born? To be loved? To be hated? No. Even in some weird, gleaming house with all the memories of her past, it never felt like she asked for any of this. She never wanted her life, her family, or even her own body during her time alive. Maybe it was the will of the gods. Maybe it was God's will that she had her life and lost it just as quickly. Or, maybe, a darker fate of cloudy days left her to suffer just for the sake of some randomness that didn't care and laughed at a hurt woman.

She finally grasped the knife. It clinked and rattled against the table before she secured it in her shaking hand. She wanted to kill. She wanted to take vengeance on the random bursting stars that gave birth to her. She didn't care if murder and blind destruction had no point. If what made her feel good shed blood, why would she care for one slip of a knife? What did it matter? Just like some stupid power that made her, what would some stupid action matter—metal through skin? She would do as she pleased. She would do what made her happy. The silver knife felt so natural in her hand.

She turned back toward her husband. He not only wanted to die by her, but at her hand, some radical acceptance of the inescapable, it could be guessed. Maybe it was the ultimate submission to love. But as much as he said he loved his wife and his son and his people and his friend, his love was only for his own life. His "love" was nothing but a blurry reflection of his own self. Flesh from dirt: this is all Jani saw in Mikalla's crying eyes. Her husband's tears were only salt and saline, not tears, just liquid. His body was no more than a bag of fruitless skin.

She hated it. And with the knife in hand, she fumed red, seeing nothing more than angry shapes around a worthless being. Kaleidoscopic red and black and red again. She ground her teeth. Her jaw scraped her front teeth.

She let out a roar that shouted from it the souls of infinite dead and suffering souls. Jani yelled in despair. She screamed and wailed like a warrior, scared of pain but not of death. Her cry was like a song from rusty nails.

She charged at the only person who loved her wholly and fully—the man who embraced even the smallest cracks in her spotless skin. But he was never the only man who lusted after her. He was not the only man to have ever wanted her. But maybe he was the only one who loved her fully.

Pain is all I feel.

She didn't have the care or the awareness to know what angered her, but her fury was deep-seated and primal, feral, thirsty for blood. But in all her rage, a picture of her son popped into vision. Coyote had her same eyes— everyone always said that. She remembered the day she bore the child. No one else delivered it. It was only her and the baby working through the suffering together when Mikalla left her alone to get help. Though her blood ran red-hot with anger, her heart calmed for a brief moment as she reminisced about the birth of her only child. She recounted the day—the moment that her only son came into the world. Through her. By her. Her eyes ceased to see as her mind lived the memory:

She lay there in her bed all those years back, countless moons ago. The only one home was Mikalla. He worked in his office while the pregnant Jani felt a flow seep onto her sheets in the dark bedroom. She thought it was a normal discharge... until it wasn't.

The fluid continued to flow from her body, almost like life force being drained from her and soaking the sheets of their bed. It ran and ran—the steady stream turned to a flood. She felt a popping sensation and then more warm fluid. She gasped in terror.

Is this happening? Am I really here? No one prepared me for—there was no one—the... oh my gods! A jolt or some kind of burn shook her all at once. She vibrated in shock watching the sheets get drenched in a river of fluid, looking down at her giant bulbous stomach.

She tried to breathe, but the terror of the image of her own body left her head in a hopeless daze. She shook; she tremored. Her legs quaked as she tried to gasp for air. Her skin ran with beads of sweat. She feared. She pained. And she only had one person to call, and she yelled out the name that could possibly relieve her of the pain.

She screeched Mikalla's name. Her voice rattled the windows and shook the curtains all around her. She yelled it again and again. "*Mikalla*!" It was the only word she could think of. It was the only word that could maybe, possibly, ease the soreness she felt ripping her insides apart.

All Jani saw was red, and all she felt were black daggers grounding her insides. She yelled, desperate for someone, *anything*, to take away the pain. It seeped through her body as her sight went splotchy, and her legs went crooked and stiff. Her torso shook as her face streamed with sweat. Fluid and panic rattled the seams of the house.

The only things throughout the house that could be heard were screams and footsteps and a distant voice as the rapid footsteps grew louder, louder. The mansion seemed so small and lonely and quiet despite the rumbling and the yelling and the giant vaulted ceilings. Jani's vision glowed and blurred. Light poured in as things darkened like an abyss. She only wished for the pain to stop. But worse than the pain was the confusion. Yes, the confusion of it all felt like a dream. She couldn't tell if this pain, this life, this time in the dark bedroom mattered at all and what it would mean for anything. If it had any meaning at all, she couldn't tell.

Mikalla rushed into the room. He nearly broke the door, the wall, and the dresser in his panic. His eyes widened at the mess on the bed; his wife's screech ticked his ears.

"Jani, Jani!"

"Mikalla.… Huh… uh… huhh."

"Jani, Jani, Jani, you're okay. It's okay." The world froze as he laid his shaking hand, lightly, lightly, on his wife's bloated belly. "You just need to relax and listen to the feelings of—"

"*Relax*," she huffed, "how... can I... *relax*?"

"Because you're strong. You'll be okay. You know how to do this already." Mikalla spoke softly with care, with whispers that sounded louder than the wind.

"No... uh... I don't."

"You do, Jani. I only need you to do one thing for me. One thing…. That's it. Okay? That's i—"

"*What*? What is it? Huh! Huh! Uhhh!" Jani yelled in pain.

"Hey, hey… hey. *Relax*. I just need you to relax," he whispered. "I just need you to relax." Mikalla's gazed at his wife with soft eyes. "I believe in you.

"*I can't!*"

"Jani, Jani…." He sought the solace of her eyes, but she glared elsewhere, looking everywhere but at her husband.

"*I c—huh! Can't*! It's coming!"

"Okay, breathe, breathe, breathe, breathe, breathe, breathe…. Just breathe with me, Jani. Baby. Jani, follow me: *breathe in…* just like this, and *out…. In—*"

"I need a doctor! Doctor! *I need a doctor.*"

"I can't leave you. I just can't."

"Get the staff. Get the… servants, then. Get anyone, Mikalla!" Jani's voice strained and groaned. Beads of sweat ran down her forehead like the fluid that filled the bed.

Mikalla yelled for the servant and screeched for him to go get a medic for Jani.

He sprinted out of the house to retrieve help. Yet by the time the medic came into the room, he was no longer needed.

Mikalla's mouth hung open at the sight. He froze motionless for a moment. The doctor looked on at the scene.

Mikalla ran quickly towards his wife and the tiny pink being that mewed out as loud as it could. "I don't think we need you anymore," Mikalla whispered to the doctor. "Please get out."

Jani did something her husband hadn't seen in a long time; she smiled. At the beauty of new life and new horizons, a wellspring of joy exploded within him, flowing out in the form of tears.

Mikalla put one hand on Jani and placed his other gentle hand on his son's soft and precious forehead. Overrun with tingling joy—not something the mere world and all its senseless cruelty could ever grant them. This *thing*, this infant, crying and pink and eyes of bright emeralds, had so much to *see*. They just created a work, a marvel, an indelible mark that could never be erased. A child. Jani sighed and caught her breath in relief. Her face glistened with sweat, and her eyes glowed as both of the proud new parents sat in awe at a creation no pen or brushstroke could ever rival. The newborn boy squealed and cooed. He looked around at a world he knew was cruel. This baby brought into the world had no choice but to leave comfort for an existence that only rewards growth and punishes with pain.

"Are we... still good with the name?" Mikalla asked. "Because he looks like a 'Coyote' to me."

Jani slowly nodded her head, too tired to cry, too tired to fight. Her exhaustion only allowed her to smile and whisper, "Yeah. Coyote. He's a 'Coyote.'"

Mikalla kissed his son's forehead for the first time in Jani's arms. A shiver ran through him. "He'll always be able to scrap for himself—in the cold and the dark…. And I already love him more than my own life."

Jani stared at her child. He continued to scream and squelch in a high pitch. And yet, all still seemed quiet and soundless. All that could be heard were Jani's words, which she desperately wanted to live on forever: "Me too. He's… beautiful." Mikalla cried and watched her grin. That was all he ever wanted for his wife. "Beautiful. More beautiful than anything."

The room lived like a ravenous flame, burning the bed and the walls, melting the house, the Inner Gardens, and all the rich nobles who lurked around with no purpose. Coyote was born into a burning earth with loving hands that would leave him soon enough. But the baby didn't know that. Maybe no one knew that. But the love that flared between the three kindled an unending blaze that would soon consume the entire kingdom, its palace, and its countless commoners. The rest of the world would look on and kneel at the light of the raging fire. The child that could be warmed by nothing was then birthed into a world that stood to burn and burn, by parents who both had scorching souls. But the gods would have it no other way.

Coyote would continue to scorch the thickets and sands of the future in order to stay warm. After all, ashes are the most fertile, the most promising grounds of all for renewed life. And the joyous couple celebrated renewed life in silent stillness. Both parents looked as one pair of eyes; they looked at the creation who changed their world forever. And, maybe, he would change the world forever, melting and molding it into his own image. But probably not.

The bundle felt so cold in her hands. She held him tighter, tearing up, letting her eyes stream, listening to the cries of Coyote ring out to the room and the world. Jani embraced her child, kissed it with all her strength, and held the baby tightly to her cheek. This entity, this being, this *person*, was hers. It was beside and out of her control, and she felt a searing pain within her emptied womb that itched urgently. The only way to scratch that itch was to hold Coyote close, kiss him softly, feed him, and be there always for him. She fought the urge with her mind, but her body overpowered any thoughts. She felt the warmth of her husband's embrace.

And, maybe, she thought, *all could be good. All could be excellent and well with this pink wonder the gods have granted us. Maybe... this feeling? What is it? Is this happiness?*

The thought of a new future—a clear horizon beset by sky and sun, a loose breeze brushing light white clouds—bright with possibilities of hope. She grinned and never thought to realize how effortless it was—to enjoy, to love, to *smile*. She didn't think about the world of dirt and blood that she brought her child into. Jani forgot for a moment all the sickness and pain on Earth and found only good in that bright baby boy. She thought only of her child, and that thought transcended all beauty and soared deeper and higher than any one pleasure she'd ever derived from anything else. Jani didn't even think to breathe as she smiled, as breathing would have taken energy away from her child, her ecstasy, her life's complete companion.

It was all so easy then. It was all right there for her, as if the whole earth and all its infinite force whispered secrets just for her. That baby wrapped in tiny pink flesh, quivering; her heart struck with a pike so venomous, the black ink filled her veins from that point on and pumped through her heart for the rest of her living life. She was struck with the awe of the gods, her body paralyzed by the poison that ate and gulped her soul. As her child came out of her, so did the significance of her power fill her bones and her heart. The sand and water and light let out their secrets then. The birth of her baby carved a distinct spot in her mind, in her flesh, in the slit of time as her existence in the universe.

The memory warmed her like a hearth of crackling flame, connected to something other than her own flesh, something beyond her. And yet, as the memories were far off in an alien world, it still felt so close to her still-beating heart.

But then she shook back in sharp pain.

The warm memory soon shattered.

Maybe it was reality, maybe another scene that was only to bleed into the next. The warmth mattered little as it all melted from her mind; it all faded away. She couldn't relive it again, or there maybe was more, or maybe there was no way to take the pain away. Maybe there was no life without pain. No matter where she was—no matter the house, the life, the existence, the room, the bed—she didn't want to be there. She didn't want to be anywhere.

She gripped the knife in all its silver splendor. The rings on her fingers and silver bracelets matched the shining dagger in her white-knuckled hand. Her breath sped up, heaving and sweating. She faced Mikalla, and they finally locked eyes. Husband and wife, two entities that walked at the same slit of time, separated by so much pain and so many lies. It all scarred both of their heavy hearts and doomed them. The same universe that birthed them never gave them a chance for them to succeed; the powers that moved the sea, wind, and stars also wanted to move them far apart once they ignited some special spark.

Jani held the knife by her side. Her arm quivered. Her jaw chattered, but she would never let her lips quiver.

Mikalla stood still and gazed into her eyes. He hoped the time would never end, leering into those emerald gems. He hoped her eyes would be the last thing he saw. He had little else to believe in at that moment, maybe ever.

But he missed his son. He couldn't do anything to get him back. He wondered and wished hopelessly for his son's success. Is that not what any father wants and wishes?

Chapter 11
A Mother's True Love

He stood cold. He stood staring at the marble. That man in fine linens seemed like nothing, only a gasp of air in the universe to an emperor that could decide anything. But as he was human, and as he stood leading countless humans, Coyote thought he may as well be among other people—the same beings that also bore his human flesh.

The emperor never desired to leave, but desire was a **stupid silly** thing!

He left to chase the soul of the kingdom through his front door.

Coyote donned his normal brown robe stinking of wine and rancid breath of poor flesh. After the cold marble of his home cooled his bones, the sun felt hot on his skin, his hands, and his face, and pressed against his feet like a hot stamp as he stepped outside. He walked past many people who looked his way and shrugged silently. Still, those people he passed by turned their heads to peer toward a man in rags while everyone else wore jewels and silk-satin.

Coyote stopped before he entered the steps down to the commons. Before he could even listen to the hum of the city's people, he heard a shrill voice yell out at him.

"Hey! Beggar! Come here! Identify yourself…."

Coyote faced away and looked at the ground. The nape of his hidden neck was cloaked in brown.

"I'm talking to you."

"Then what do you have to say?"

"What was that?"

Coyote turned around and faced the person yelling at him. Clearly, the ragged emperor realized this was a privileged man of noble birth, softened by a secluded culture that coddled his mind to only think one way. This man had never had a sense of lack, and so instead he had to seek it out on his own accord, driving wedges in between him and the rest of the massive society of "others" he looked down upon. Coyote looked on at the man, not backing away, not walking toward him—the emperor stood still and poised in the face of certain scrutiny.

After seeing the emperor's face, the noble man could not be bothered with dirtying his silk dress by taking a knee. Instead, he recognized Coyote's face of stone, widened his eyes, and quickly scampered away—as if running from the sun or some other great and unmistakable force of the universe. He ran away quickly, while still knowing it was pointless and futile to do so. The damage had already been done. Although this nobleman in silk knew that the emperor was a weird hermit, he wasn't *so* stupid to think that the emperor wasn't smart or able to remember a face.

Coyote turned back towards his goal of descending into the commons and to chase the soul of the kingdom he now ruled—the last soul he felt was worth saving. His father's words and his mother's kisses played endlessly through his head and stuck like needles all over his body, all the time and at every waking hour while the sun still glared. His whole heart carried a sack of stone that dragged behind him and slowed every step he took forward. And yet, he took those steps. Down every stair, past every gate and checkpoint, and of course, without any accompanying soldiers to safeguard his wellbeing.

He was better off alone. Just as he was born that way, he would die that way, and even among people, loneliness seemed to be his only guard, his only friend, his only guide, his only whim.

He went past the gate away from the Inner Gardens, away from the opulence and lavish people, lavish parties, all of the glitz, and the silken robes of the drones at bay always. He needed something new; even an old soul needed something new.

And so he descended. He went down the steps past the guards and the sentinels and soldiers staring at him. "Sir, do you need someone to accompany you?"

"No. Go. I am me. That's enough, just as much as you are enough. Stay at your post."

He went down the steps and left all his insidious memories behind. His body felt lighter as he kept descending, going down, down every step, every stair into a denser air, a thick air filling his nostrils and ears. It all hummed then. It all reminded him of years lost behind as he lost everything. But losing everything, possibly, made him gain the world and its many secrets whispering in his ear as he smiled just a bit. A smug crescent tightened across his worn young face. He was excited—excited to feel the bite of pain once again, the threat of violence once again, the excess of less, the fatigue of a lesser life full of more, once more, maybe.

Maybe.... He thought to himself.

The stairs were dirty and jagged. But with every step, the raucous commons of the city filled the ears of Coyote and made him smile—smile more, smile yet again for the first time in years.

Well, for a time, he'd been wanting to go down into the commons to see how his people worked and walked; *he wanted to see how the people lived.* But to this point, he'd always felt like they weren't his people. But slavery or not, people had to belong to something else, and the young emperor knew that finally he had subjects to which he was beholden.

His simple story wanted to be the greatest ever told. Young men always wanted to be the... ugh, it doesn't matter. But maybe it mattered.

He finally made his way to the bottom of the stairs with his hood up and his ears open to the sounds and sights of the city. He inhaled with his full lungs the scent of the city as he found himself on the equal earth that all his subjects walked upon every day. His scruffy face was barely visible. He could not be recognized, but he worried less about that and more about what others did. It was as if Coyote was only a soul to be filled by other powers. He was merely an empty cup—his mind, his heart, his eyes, his flesh waiting to be filled with something fresh and clean—waiting to be born again.

Coyote looked around and saw the same pictures he expected to see in a bustling city—people walking, running, hustling, yelling, sounds from the heart and from the throat, and slick words thrown from the throne of the brain. But what good was a brain? What good was anything if the wind and sand and water and heat always prevailed in the void?

Coyote's constant search for meaning in his mind decayed his soul over time, trying to rationalize all his life the pain and loss that tore at him when he woke, and each sleepless night his reddened eyes stayed wide open and gazing, staring into a ceiling that barred his eyes from the stars.

Coyote walked on in his own city, slowly swiveling his head, squinting his eyes to watch out for anything and everything that could *mean* something to him. *But meaning was a fickle and stupid thing.* The young emperor shunned all his useless spiritual and philosophical thoughts to the side in favor of his five senses as he explored the city he inherited deeply. He didn't look to make an impact on this journey among his people; he sought to see how his impact influenced every soul and set of eyes in the busy streets of the kingdom that constantly teetered on the stories they were told.

Simply, Coyote wanted to see what these people believed in, and their actions would inform the emperor of their philosophies without them knowing. Coyote was a rag-ridden spy cloaked in an unassuming robe, masked by a beard and sad eyes that served as windows to his freezing heart.

And so he walked on and looked to study more, to feel more, to dive deeper into the finest crevices of the beautiful souls that comprise the kingdom, *his* kingdom—humanity.

Have my stories had any meaning? Have my actions ever had any impact that does something or moves anything? Coyote asked himself cutting questions as he always did.

The young emperor walked on and thought of evil and death and how gray clouds may choke his life out at any time.

He saw a woman with curls in her black hair, taking her child by the hand and leading her away from the bustling streets. Coyote turned his head and trailed the mother like a magnet to metal. He followed her at a distance, just close enough to watch her admonish her child, gripping her wrist tighter as she yanked her away from the crowd, away from the rest, long gone from the masses. She dragged her young daughter—who was small but could walk and talk like her mother—toward her house, presumably.

But Coyote squinted through the thinning crowd and tiptoed as the streets narrowed and silenced. He lagged behind the mother and daughter as the noise lessened and the serenity of silence took over. The green of lush grass overtook the street. The crows of the crowd and peeps of people seeped into the whistle of birds in the open air. A field crept under the feet of the mother and the daughter as she lessened her grip on her precious child. The young girl slipped from the grasp and twirled around, looking everywhere. Coyote caught a glimpse of a smile—yes, a smile—the wonderment of a child new to a world that opened itself. Coyote watched what he thought was a cruel world embrace a hopeful child. Maybe children were a simple way to a happier future. Coyote didn't know. And he never knew anything.

He saw something as he kept watching. He saw something change—not the grip of the mother, but rather her attitude. She didn't pursue her child as the girl with dark hair slid away from her mother and trotted into the grassy plains beyond—far beyond—the city walls. It was beyond the state, the grasp of the guards, the pull of the people, and the influence (maybe) of the emperor.

Coyote witnessed something he had never seen. He wondered if it had happened before or if it would ever happen again. He watched with a wide jaw, steady eyes, and a still body.

The mother said something to her daughter that Coyote would never forget: "Go and leave and be by yourself. Return when you do, and I will embrace you. Stay out in the wilderness, and I will miss you. But I will love you as you go on and find the snags of the roots and the sticks of certain thorns. I will rejoice in your bloody bare toes and the cuts that don your face. Your journey is your life, no longer a part of me but always a part of my heart. Every lonely step you take on your own through the jagged rocks will always be towards bright heavens."

"And what if I step on a thorn, Momma?"

"Then you get hurt and bleed."

"And what if I get hurt without you? Can I call for you? What happens then?" The young girl's face puffed with redness. "When I fall? When I'm hurt, Momma? Will you hear me?" The girl cried as she looked toward thick thickets and dark caverns draped in canopies of giant leaves.

Her mother stood there still as her daughter walked forward. The girl felt the grass. Fear stroked her soft face, her bright eyes glazed over as her red lips formed into a frown. Fear, mortal fear, flushed her flesh, turning crystal-pale. Her head bobbed up and down as she stared at the ground. What once looked like bright green plains filled with grass growth and healthy hedges now all looked brown to the girl like a gray sheet pulled the blue of the sky away. She saw through the many blades of grass then; she saw what the flowers and towering trees grew from:

earth. She whispered to herself as her eyebrows melted into deadened eyes, traumatized. "Momma?" She spread the grass out and stared at the black dirt that had always remained hidden from her. She loved the plants, not the dirt. She closed her eyes and tried not to cry. The picture in her head showed the passing of time that turned the rich soil to sand. Green to yellow, and then soon all would be black, as the picture faded and all went void. "*Momma…?*" All went dark for the girl with the thin lips—black sun that nourished the black dirt she stood on. She fixed her sad gaze toward her mother.

They looked at one another, still and silent, so only wind was heard. Only the breeze could be felt. Coyote could only make out the girl's crying eyes, as her mother's back was turned away from him.

"Momma… why?" Sadness bled into rage, but fear ruled over all her face and small body full of life, young vitality of red blood that pumped so quickly through tiny angry veins. "Momma! What are you—why are you doing this? *I don't understand*!"

Coyote thought of the girl, her galactically complex mind being reduced to the base human urges of fear. A complete grayness passed by her eyes in place of redness and swelling. This would not be the last time she would cry. But they would be the richest tears she would ever shed as she thought about all the thorns she would step on.

Her mother remained silent and still, hiding under her hood and watching the girl explore a new world, a darker world of dirt. Her daughter sat on the ground amidst the tall grass so only her confused, scared, blood-red eyes could be seen.

But what was one more salty tear that fell to the unliving dirt? What was the strength and struggle of a lone child shoved into the natural world? Was this the society he inherited or the culture he created? Did any of it matter? Maybe it mattered.

"Why? Momma…."

The mother finally broke her cold silence and spoke. "You need to understand that for yourself." And although frozen in a standing statue pose, Coyote heard the woman sniffle loudly after she said this. Her voice wavered just a bit before turning back to a cold, stoic, icy rhythm of speech. "You have to find the meaning on your own—the meaning of all of it. Why does the grass you pull from the ground grow as tall as it can before shrinking back to brown? Why do trees spend their whole lives shooting upward, taking all the air, sun, and water they can, just to get big and beautiful, only to wither away to a sad, old stump? Why are you scared to leave what you've always known? Why are you scared to get hurt? You're going to get hurt, and your body doesn't like that. Your bones don't want to feel it. You don't feel alone when you run by yourself in the plains when you know I will always be there. Yet you are still by yourself, Aaliyah. You've always been by yourself. It's only been you, and I love you. I love you more than I want to breathe. But love is hard; it's not easy, Aaliyah. True love never is. Beauty isn't easy to reach, My Love."

At this point, the mother began to weep, and the daughter she called Aaliyah also cried with her. The woman stayed still while the girl ran back to her and, with open arms, hugged her mother and held on. She squeezed the larger body with her smaller arms, and they both wept together. "What if I get thirsty?"

"Then the water will be sweet, and you'll feel great when you quench that thirst... because I know you will."

"Momma! I don't wanna go! I don't wanna leave you!"

Coyote was puzzled. He'd never studied such an elaborate scheme of nature's forces. He couldn't figure if this was natural or if this mother was completely against all of history.

They both wept heavy tears. They sniffled and sobbed.

The great, poor emperor squinted his eyes and twisted his face. *Is this beautiful?*

"Momma...."

Silence and the chirps of birds flirted with swift wind. All stood still despite the leaves and animals quivering constantly.

All stood still as they continued to weep together. Red inflamed their throats and flooded their eyes.

"Momma, why do you want to hurt me?"

They sniveled sadly. Still wind in the sun. The breeze spoke for a while before the mother could collect the tears she shed.

"I would never hurt you. I never want to hurt you.... The world does. There are thorns on the bushes you want to touch and snakes in the grass where you want to tread. The snakes want your life. The thorns want your blood. The rivers and fresh streams will only dry you up."

The girl curled up into a ball, shaken by the words of the wind, the ways of the world, and the tears of her mother. *Parents aren't supposed to cry in front of their children, right*? Coyote shivered. The breeze seemed to go right through his bones.

"Momma, why wouldn't you protect me from the snakes? Why do they have to be there? Why does it have to be this way?"

"I can't protect you from them. But when faced with the cruelty of this world, Aaliyah, I want you to face it on your own, so that one day, maybe, you may master the venomous strikes of the snakes and the thorns of the bloody rosebushes and the cold pellets of rain that will chill you to the bone."

They sniffled and cried together. The weary emperor, in all his years, never saw a soldier with a grip as strong as the woman who held her daughter as tenderly as she did.

Coyote nodded slowly. He realized those words were his effect on the kingdom. He tightened his hood and turned back home without a second glance.

His walk back to his house was brief as he rushed past so many people and never looked up once. He stumbled and fell and crept back up to his feet. He was now on a mission, a man who built his own purpose. Beautiful. It was all beautiful, even if he had to hurt others to get what he wanted.

Oh! It was a sweet perfume that resounded from the dying rose petals like a chorus of decay! What a symphony.

The young man barreled back to his home. He trampled through the woods and past thorns, seeing through rabid eyes rabbit ears in the bushes and then people all going one way or another in groups like fish. He had something to write down. The emperor had something to say, but the only way to have everyone hear it was to say it alone on an empty page.

Chapter 12

A Lost Love Found

Far before he was a man with any power, Coyote—the one with the boyish face and dirty robe and bright smile—once fell in love with a girl named Metzli. He loved her from afar, loved her without a word. He would only ever want her affection. Her passionate grasp would be his gold.

She was new life to him. To her, he was useful— just maybe useful.

The girl with green catlike eyes spent her days selling bread for coins and avocado for extra money. But the poor boy had nothing to sell and nothing to buy anything with. He only had a love for the girl that plenty filled his empty stomach. And he loved her without a word. He smiled at her beauty from afar through the crowd, a big stupid grin at some girl he didn't know. It was as if the gods granted her a sacred light from the sky inexplicably, an angel in the human sense, and yet she was far and above the greatest little human he had ever seen. The boy traveled lightly after his bag was stolen—a drifting-dirty vagabond. His empty hands held no coins; they presented barren skin of pale palms. But, for some reason, the girl saw a spark, a glint in the boy—his eyes, his naive face, his sad, searching flesh—and she gave him a loaf of bread without asking for anything in return. And he loved her even more. He thanked the gods with every glance he got to throw her way. She was his world, his goal, his highest aim. She shone brightly in simple, clean spotless robes, and her smile—oh! Her smile! It lit the sky and gave the sun its life, proof of the gods themselves.

But that was long ago. Maybe the girl named Metzli liked Coyote and his face and his innocent questions. She was a worker from a young age who toughened by bargaining in the city with money-hungry,

hungry commoners who needed both bread and gold. But the boy seemed to have no attachment to anything in particular, the sad-eyed, sullen one who stood out from the rest with his silk speech and soft touch. Maybe she pitied him—not as a person, but as a child—despite them being the same age. Maybe she pitied him. Maybe she liked him. Maybe her fine filaments within her lower loins quivered a slit when he spoke or smiled with his thin lips and bright eyes.

There was a time—a brief and fleeting time—when Metzli wanted to care for the ragged boy with the clean teeth and the dirty clothes. A gritty body encased a spotless soul she wanted to have in her. She wanted it—*him*—inside her. It was a delicate dance, and her bright body knew all the steps.

There was a time when they connected and felt each other. They both wanted to connect more. There was a time when frescos of Metzli's glowing skin, face, cat-shaped eyes, and careful hands of a goddess ran through Coyote's young mind. But sometimes, young minds were wisest.

There was a time when Coyote and Metzli were in love but hopelessly apart. Both their hearts sank every step away. The night felt colder to the boy in the robes and the girl with coins to collect without the other.

They were in love. Whatever love meant, they felt the flame of it, the heat of the hungry-hot orange spill that ravaged hearts and devoured everyone and everything and all hearts and minds and flesh and couples and romances and true love and cheating and infidelity and souls of wanderlust wanting something more…. They too would be devoured by the flame of "*love*." Oh, ugh, ha! *Love*.

Metzli and Coyote—there was a time when they looked to one another with a shared future in mind. The girl and the boy wanted more than just to hug or touch. They both wanted the soul. They wanted the body—not the part, but the whole.

"You're a strange boy, Coyote. But I wouldn't expect you to understand something you've never had to work for."

Coyote held back the tears. *Those green eyes. Those golden looks. That smile… those* cheeks. *She'll never be mine.* He hid his face from the girl and lowered his cracked voice.

"You know, I could take you back there one day."

"To the Inner Gardens?"

"To it all. I could take you past the gate and we could look at the statues and bathe in gold. I could take you to the royal palace so you could meet my mentor, King Oro."

She jumped back as her jaw dropped. "You know the *king?*"

"He's my only friend. And I left him. And I left my mother, and she lives in a house larger than this entire plaza. That's where I've laid my head my entire life."

"How could you not be happy?" The girl asked. "You're *rich.* Why would you leave that? How could you turn your back on such a life?"

"I'm turning my back on something else. I'm turning my back on darkness. All the gold that shimmers under the sun couldn't outshine the dark forces and confusion I've felt my entire life. I... can't really explain it."

"I don't understand you, Coyote. But where are you going next?"

"Wherever the gods sway the winds, I guess."

"Hmph. Gods. You still believe in them? Look around." She stretched her arm out, revealing the marvelous constructions all around the city of Idaza—bridges and buildings and roads and cars. "Believe in this. Don't believe in the silly *gods*."

"Can I ask you something, Metzli?"

"Sure."

"When was the last time you did something for yourself—not for progress, not for money, not for the kingdom, but for yourself?"

Silence. A long pause pervaded the biting wind as Coyote turned around to face her again. He looked into her eyes and he felt somehow like he had control of the girl. Like he had earned something from her, about her, because of her. Even the air around her glowed as she stood, still-faced, looking back at Coyote and his huge hood.

"Like what would that be? What could I do for myself?"

He felt right then the path he must travel. But in his weak and sensitive mind, all he could think about was the girl—her look, her figure, staring back in amazement. And with those same conflicting thoughts crashing against one another, they broke the dam of tears in his eyes which he needed to choke back in front of her. He tried with all his might not to cry and hoped that the shroud of night could hide his stark red eyes.

But those days of love were eclipsed by loss. And his red eyes stayed still and dry like sandpaper behind his skull, missing the girl and her touch. His sore red eyes still dug in the back of his head for memories he would love to forget, past attachments he would love to forget. But she was a part of him—like an arm, a kidney, an eyeball.

But he couldn't forget. Even as his boyish face turned pale and nervous and scruffy over the years, he couldn't forget what that first girl did to him. She was supposed to be the innocent girl with bread to sell and eyes that revealed heaven itself; she had that one soft touch to heal all his sickness. With her, Coyote could feel whole. He seemed to have seen through the girl, her bones, her skin, through her stark, bright eyes, a soul that whispered sweetness. She held his key to honey and all things golden somewhere inside her keep. He wanted, *needed*, that key. His spine and skin thirsted for all the secrets he needed to learn from hers, *so what was a mind to a body? What was a simple boy's brain to do with a body that wanted and lusted? Go along with it. Go along, and by all means, go along.* Get swept up in the torrent and feel nothing chasing that torrent, madly, viciously, and with no regard for a thing else.

The very moment he laid eyes upon her was the beginning to the end of his life. So as he saw a new horizon within the girl, his clock started to tick with the stink of death. And the death only reeked more with every second that and sun that passed by. It was all a charade of shadows he wanted to grab. It was all a parade of puppets he wanted to be a part of. And he would never get what he wanted.

But the girl? What did she think? Well, unlike the boy, she *actually thought*. She calculated and looked inside herself, unlike the boy her age who only pictured things and conjured up fantasies in his dim mind, lit by candles and fickle flames.

Metzli had the foresight for a great investment: the girl gave the boy a loaf of bread for the chance to have access to untold riches—gold and silver and gems of all kinds. All she needed to do was be kind and smile and give him a little in hopes he would give her a lot.

But there was another hope in the girl's investment. Her calculation also had another variable; she liked him. She liked the way his eyebrows and lips moved. She liked how he spoke so innocently, curious with the thoughts of a naive child ripe for adventure. He needed to work and get hurt. He needed to feel the sting of society like she had—or so that's what she thought.

They both wanted each other. The only thing that lied between the boy and the girl were hundreds of miles and many reasons. So they could do it, right? If only one day they could be together…. They believed in secret that they could be together without knowing anything but their desires.

Both Coyote and Metzli were not like most people. They lived by their wants, not their needs, but they thought their desires were their needs. It was deluded and psychotic teenage magic, and it all worked so well. Their love sparked for a tiny tick of time so vast it engulfed their whole lives. The air that made their breath would carry their story forever.

But the boy turned his back on the girl as he put his hood on and walked away with a tear in his eye. He waned on toward a destiny untold. He didn't know what moved him, but even though he was on fire for Metzli, he wanted to discover that fire within himself first before going back to the girl with the green eyes.

But the story went awry as he lost his footing and lost his way and let all his loved ones slip through his hand like grains of sand. The boy only grew more aimless as he wandered while time went on. He didn't even know what his words meant to the people.

At least Metzli knew what she desired. Metzli knew what she wanted, and she always went for it. She never hesitated to welcome Lupus' advice and encouraging words. The High Priest of Idaza seemed to believe in *her*, the simple girl from the commons who had only willpower and, through sheer grit, breached the high walls of the Inner Gardens to enjoy a life of splendor and wealth she's always dreamed of. And she fought her whole life, taught her whole life by her working parents to work harder and never stop.

And so, when greeted with the chance for ultimate power, she would not stop pursuing the great, good goal that lay in front of her. And in between her and the mist storm of power was a giant wooden barrier that made a sinking sound every time her knuckles rapped against it.

She knocked on the door again.

She waited for a while, shivered, and knocked again. She tried to speak, but another shiver in the wind made her body tremble in the presence of the house that seemed so much larger than the royal palace despite its smaller stature, filled with so much more life despite its emptiness.

While she waited and tried to keep from shivering, Metzli tried to speak, but while her mouth moved, her "hello" was swept away into the afternoon air. She tried to think her way out of anxiety, but her creeping train of thought only led her to more towering conclusions….

It's all in your head, Metzli. There's no special presence here—just a man you met long ago. He's human; he's just like you and Lupus and the rest of the nobility, right?

In a dim and dusty room above, a nervous man could only hear his own steps despite the voice from below. His ears and eyes seemed to be shrouded in a haze that could only recall shadows of the memory of his mother.

The young, young man paced and kept his hood on. He twiddled his fingers and muttered to himself. He needed to be bathed. He needed to be touched, talked to, and *loved*. But he forsake all his needs and took shelter in his own mind; the constant cloud that hung over him reigned. He shut out all sounds from outside his own bubble of existence, safe within the shroud of his robe's warm hood, safe in the dust of the room he'd always known. He didn't want to hear anything. He didn't want to be anything.

"Coyoteeeee!"

His servant hollered from the foyer.

The Emperor of Idaza just kept pacing. He kept his eyes on the ground, head down, his vision obscured by the sides of his hood. He heard something and listened to nothing but the wailing of space; he so wanted to shut out of his ears and eyes. Maybe a distraction could keep him from the depths that lurked and laughed beneath his hazy thoughts.

"Coyoteeeeee! Someone knocks for you...."

"And who is it?"

"She's, erm, a noble lady... a maiden... a—"

"Well, what is it? Spit it out!"

"She's a... girl. A woman in black. And she knocks for you."

"Ask—" Coyote realized he hadn't breathed for a while. He took a step forward and rolled his shoulders, straightening his back. He inhaled. He exhaled. He calmed himself. "*Ask* what she knocks for, please." The Emperor of Idaza was clearly rattled. His eyes twitched and fidgeted. He played with his fingers. His face fidgeted nervously.

"Well, My Lord, she knocks for you."

"Identity? What's her identity? Who is she?"

"She says she's been a key member in the royal court for years now. She says she met you when you were young. She said that, that—"

"That what?"

"That she knew you... that she *knows* you—that she knows you personally, My Lord."

In the young emperor's mind flashed past snapshots of pain, trauma, and beauty. He could still feel it all at full force—the pain of losing his grip on a future, some bright tulip within a hungry jungle. He forever felt the pull of her flower—he knew what girl knocked at his door.

His feeble fists tightened. "I don't want to talk to her."

"My Lord, she seems very insistent on speaking with you—"

"I don't want to talk to her. Tell her to leave. Go! Go and do it!"

The young emperor heard mumbling from upstairs. The servant said something. The woman said something. Coyote twitched at the sound of her voice. He couldn't make out her words but could feel her tone. The house vibrated with life, with something unseen that echoed off the walls and ceilings. *Only memories…. They're only memories, and memories are nothing. They're figments, and they're fake, and they're misgiven. Mistakes. Mistakes! All of my memories are all mistakes. They're all fake.*

The young man tightened his hood. He put both hands to his face and shriveled and shivered. Stomach churned green, gut flipped and inflamed. He doubled over in imaginary pain. Maybe he should've thought about that.

Meanwhile, at the entrance of the mansion, the servant spoke to Metzli, who had grown so much since the world always changed. She wore an all-black suit that pressed tightly. The servant needed to get rid of her but also wanted her to stay.

"So there's *nothing* you can do for me to talk to the emperor?"

"Well, there *are* things I could do, Ma'am. However, I am unable to bring you to him at the moment. I need you to please lea—"

"So there *is* something you can do? What's your name, anyway?"

"Oh! I'm—well, that's not important. The emperor is busy with important administrative work for the foreseeable future."

"Did you know he sent for me?"

"I—I don't think that's the case, Ma'am. I apologize sincerely; I really do!"

"So you're calling me a liar?"

"I'm sorry... I need a moment, please." The servant slammed the door on the woman and looked unsolved. He huffed and ran up the grand staircase.

"Um, sir, Master, she seems to be here on business, and... she said that you... *called for her*."

"Lies. It's all lies." Coyote grated his teeth and howled at the barren ceilings of his childhood home. "*Lies*! It's all a facade! A fake!" He huffed and whiffed on air, red-faced. "She's... *lying*."

"Understood, Master. However, she seemed pretty convinced that you wanted her here. She's still at the doo—"

"Everyone is convinced of their own petty delusions. She's deluded; she doesn't have an idea of what she speaks of. She's lost—just like the memories of the past. They wave in the wind and have no bearing on the earth or the people on it. She's *lost*. Lost!"

The servant found some rush of restlessness in his heart that pumped lustful life through veins, some strength, some vitality that made him sink to a black depth and a rising horizon that deepened his voice. "What if she's not lying, Coyote? What if you're the one that's fooling yourself?"

Coyote took a deep breath. His lungs searched for life or some clearing in his mind that made any sense. He looked down at the man who he trusted to hire. He was in his own house and at the whim of the emperor, but he was a human with his own will too. "I'm a lot of things, Maximus... and I may be a fool. I may be mistaken, then. I may be.... Sometimes, I feel like I don't really know anything. The lifeless sands in the desert wind know more than I do. The sun is wiser. The waters of the rivers and lakes are stronger. The mountains are prettier. I am only flesh in flesh in flesh among all the beauty and wisdom of the wider world that towers over all of us. So," Coyote said, speeding up his breath and speaking softly, moving quicker and widening his eyes, jerking his head from left to right, "I don't really know anything. What makes you think I can fool myself without knowing anything in the first place? It's sinister. It's blackmail. It's *stupid*! Who cares what she thinks or what she wants? I'm the *emperor*! I traveled far and wide so my words could reach the depths of the soul of the many… and I was chosen *from birth*! And who was I chosen by? Well, who cares and what does it matter? *I decide everything I think*! I decide everything that I am, no matter how tall the mountains may be or how much life the sun gives, I can walk and strut and swing and climb and gnash and find any way I want among all these broken paths! Understand? Is that understood?"

Maximus the servant held his single index finger up to the emperor. He took a long, deep, drawn-out inhale. The servant's lungs expanded with his eyes closed for a long moment. He meant every word he said. His throat tightened, and his gut went green. He would speak out against the reason of a person who had inherited the world and stood above it with reproach and illness. His mouth went dry, and he seemed to float in other worlds and not even see where he was or who was in front of him, lost in a glaze of clouds. But the servant had something to say, and so he spoke what dwelt on his mind as his boss taught him for years. "But, Sir, maybe you do care. Maybe she—for better or for worse—does spark a special emotional reaction from you. I could be wrong, and please forgive me if I am, but it seems like she means something to you, My Lord. It… seems like… you—"

"Spit it out, Maximus."

"It seems like you *care*."

Coyote ripped his hood off and sprinted down the stairs toward the woman in black. Something set up a cosmic collision larger than both of those tiny bodies, those tiny ideas: the idea of the dichotomy between woman and man. Their attractions and their contempt—what did it matter? Coyote seemed to think it mattered a lot as he shuttled down the stairs, barreling toward the girl, who was now a woman. His whole body shuddered as he approached the door.

He readied his throat to yell. Maximus—his family's faithful servant for decades—shouted to Coyote from upstairs to calm down. But plebians of the poor in spirit only fanned the flame that raged in Coyote's eyes.

A beautiful woman with a slight sensible smile and sentient-bright eyes stood in his giant doorway. She shined radiantly despite her black suit absorbing the sun's generous rays.

"Why are you here?"

"I'm here just to talk…. That's all."

"And talk about what?" Coyote shrilled like a rabid animal.

Metzli already knew what she wanted to say, and she had an ephemeral feeling for the man; she knew he could control him. She felt she could tie him to a string and puppet his every word in front of any crowd of any size. Metzli thought this broken young man could be pieced back together in her own image (*or, in Lupus' image*). She paid measured attention to his every twitch and tone. She saw a horizon of possibilities in the power of the puppy-like boy, and it all excited; it gave her a warm feeling that crackled just underneath her skin. Her smile was so soft and sharp at its edges. Her eyes gleamed like emeralds in the yellow sun.

"About *you*…. I want to talk about *you*, Coyote."

And there was a tiny piece of the emperor that begged him to think. *If you don't ever trust anyone, how will you ever be with anyone?*

"Why would you want to talk about or... why would you want to do that?" Coyote felt the urge to run away and sink into the earth forever. Blackness could be all he could see right then. Fears of wolves and evil reared their heads again. He tensed up at the sights of beetles and bugs slurping up his flesh forever in Hell. All those bugs would eat hungrily until they reached the bone, and then they'd gnaw at his bones until they burped and died from the time that passed.

Metzli smelled Coyote's fear. She smiled a bit more. "I want to talk to you, Coyote, because... well, I don't really know how to put it into words. I can't speak properly about what I've been feeling lately." She looked down at the ground and shuffled her feet. To Coyote, she looked innocent and vulnerable.

"What do you feel?"

"I feel... for *you*, Coyote. I *still* feel for you. I—I thought I would shake these stupid thoughts. But I kept seeing you, you! In my dreams, when I closed my eyes, and whenever I took a break from life. And then I realized,

Coyote, that you've always been the one for me. You've always been a part of me."

His jaw tightened. He growled and whispered and muttered angrily under his breath. "*Liar.*"

"What was that?"

"I said you're a *liar*!"

Metzli's green eyes widened slightly. "I'm really sorry, My Highness, but I'm afraid I don't understand. I just don't understand how you could possibly think how I'm lying about my own feelings. My own thoughts, Coyote. Could you speak, maybe, as to why—"

"I said 'liar!' You're a liar! Get out at once. Leave right now! I don't want you here and, frankly, the kingdom would be better without you in it."

Any other living being in the kingdom would've felt a flutter of fear at those words from a man so powerful at the helm of a nation so great. But Metzli—Metzli was undeterred, unshaken. She stayed calm and resolute in the face of the emperor's threat. She had not yet met the man, but she knew the boy, and to know the boy was to understand the man. The emperor was only a shell—yes, a shell—who encased the true spirit that burned bright underneath the dim crust of age and misfortune. She still thought he could reach him. She still thought she could raise him and sculpt him effectively.

But somehow, he still has those boyish eyes…. Even that weathered young man has so much life to pass on. I see it in his eyes, and I can feel every fear…. Oh, a man of power he is!

"Maybe the kingdom would be better without me here; maybe you'd feel safer—"

"It's not about safety. I fear nothing. I especially don't fear you. And it's not a kingdom, it's an empire."

"And yet, you dread every step you take, Coyote. You *are* scared. And if you claim to fear nothing at all, then I fear for you... and for your own sake." Metzli took on a motherly tone. She tilted her head to the side. She held the same pose of the face that quivered Coyote's heart long ago. Maybe a tickle. Maybe he felt a flicker from her puckered red lips. Metzli could only hope to move him somehow in a little way as women do. She could move a man to move a mountain. Those words she spoke of 'long ago' didn't seem so distant anymore when she was right there. "And still, Coyote, you sit or pace all day here in the dust, waiting for the sun to crackle into pink powder, only to wait for nightfall's painful end for it to get lit up once more. You pace underneath the cosmos you can't control, the gods who get what they want, and you only look up at what's above. You see the stars you can't reach and you fear one falling on your foot, yet you stand on top of a great nation as the head of a limitless body. It's an earthly body, but a *powerful* one, Coyote. It's a mass of spirits— so many *beautiful beings*! And I know you want them all to be free—free of their shackles. Maybe you don't yet know what imprisons your people, Coyote, and yet you search on like a brave pioneer. With enough courage and the willingness to look down from where you perch and focus on what is already in your hands, maybe you can— you *will*—discover the secrets to your kingdom! It can all be yours, Coyote. Brave Coyote…. A passionate boy turned into a man of so much resolve. The hearts and minds of the people—the unimaginable, unconquerable, indefatigable spirit of life—are all there! I realize it now! You are the bravest one among us, Coyote, and that's why I want to be right there with you, next to you, on you, alongside your journey step by step. I've missed you, My Love. I've always known you'd be the one for me. It's all right there—at your feet and in your hands—your real flesh! Your bones, my skin, a woman's lash, a child's smile—they are all your playthings! You're an emperor, Coyote. But you grew wise and yet so unwell…. The plague of the past seems to have gripped your spirit, unfortunately. But that *spirit* is such a handsome spirit, Coyote. And you've grown to be such a handsome man. And your eyes still speak of so much wonder despite all you've suffered. I know you have joy somewhere in there, somewhere deep down within you, within *maybe* the people you want to win over. And the people already love you, my handsome emperor—they just don't know that it's *you*; it's all been *your own words…* this *whole* time. *You….*" And then the woman approached him, slowly tiptoeing and taking a great deal of care to not move too much or be too heavy with her feathering feet. She felt a slight spark, some heat to the bottom of her torso that made her tremble—if only invisibly. She felt a touch, a tickle.

But the emperor somehow still loomed large over her like a great shadow. His eyes clenched tighter than his fists. He focused on her. Every strand of light that trickled through the windows seemed to darken. "I need you out of here. I need you out of here at once. Maximus will escort you out, and if you refuse or so much as twitch in any other direction other than *out* and away from me, then… I will…

oh, I can't say what I'd do to you. But whatever I would do if you disobeyed my command would be made legal because I say it is." Coyote looked toward a phantom distance past the woman and toward some unreachable past he couldn't grasp. His memories bubbling like hot stew only stirred his emotions angrier. But he spoke calmly. "Go now, or else nothing will be able to save you. You will reach the deepest lurch of pain and scream like an animal—*except*! Except there will be no one to hear your calls. The jungle will eat your body before the ground withers away. Your spirit will break and then break again. You'll wish a thousand times for oblivion, begging and pleading, but it will never come." Coyote turned his back and fixed his hood to hide the tear in his eye. He cleared his throat. Metzli could see him wiping his crying eyes from behind. "Go. Be gone."

The frozen young emperor listened to the door slam and watched Metzli through the window scuttle away from his house. He shuddered and felt a tone of heat and pressure at the sight of the back of the girl who would never love him and never did, leaving once again. But it wouldn't be the last time.

He had no wine or tobacco, nothing to drink or to smoke. His mind closed to a single dark path with no light. People were like animals. Or maybe people were animals; maybe the emperors of people were the same as the poor and the powerless. Still, he was angry and wanted revenge against the dirt and the stars. He wanted to kill the sky, his blood hotter than the stars.

Coyote just wanted some alcohol and tobacco, some pipe or cigar, something smoked or drunk that could calm his nerves.

He yelled for help. Coyote was still just a puppy as he yelped into the dark window into the coming night. His body yearned for a drink that could soothe his lips and a pipe that could put his lungs at ease. He wanted—if only for a moment—to feel nothing at all. But he had none of that. Instead of drugs and alcohol that could soothe his tightly knotted nerves, he had only his fist that banged loudly and splintered his banister. His vocal cords strained and shook the walls of the house, ne'er reaching an ear outside his own house. He shrieked into the night, wondering why he was born. But his words reached no ear.

He watched her leave over and over again through red eyes, tinting a world so awry and twisted. It was all so evil.

She kept walking and disappeared into the polluted air of the Inner Gardens. He wanted her there. Or maybe he hated her and never wanted Metzli the person, but rather some fixture of a woman that could never exist.

The young emperor's mind lamented images of the precious past. He held the brighter moments of old as pearly pictures, carefree times without struggle before he became some hopeless soul traveling quickly to the bottom of the pit. *But I see things as they are now. I have for so long…. I know the true nature of earth. This world does not like decadence. It despises those that seek to control it and its creations. I don't know about the gods. I don't know what makes life tick and tremble with vitality…. But… but I've seen life end. Lots of precious life was lost before my eyes. I know nothing about life, but all my life I've known decay and death. That—yes, that—must be the thing I'm most familiar with. That must be my strength. That must be my destiny—to bring the inevitable into my own hands. Yes, I'll have to be inevitable. It is the only way. Not for darkness, not for light—these are merely concepts. I will bring death to those who deserve it because it is what I can do, and volition is my final and only answer. What can I dominate in life if not life itself? And what is the only way to dominate life? End it. I am only doing the job I was chosen to do. I am merely doing my duty.*

Coyote drew a deep breath. He listened to his servant breathe too, inhaling heavily as if he were just in a fight, scampering in the night. This natural red fury came about him and boiled his blood; his nerves twitched under his skin. Some will to power came alive inside of him, even if in a creeping and unconscious way. The young emperor crept on clouds atop his house, his lone servant, and the entire world. And with the world at the clutch of his fingers, he chose to squeeze and grip his whole hand; he chose to lose control. Violence. *But there is no violence,* Coyote thought. *There is only matter—only small people like me going about their day and doing the best they can.*

There is only matter and the transition of particles in an indifferent world. I—for some reason—have influence over more of these particles than most of the rest. I will do what I want, not what I must. There is no obligation for a piece of the universe, and, therefore, the universe in whole has no say in what I do. I do what I do. They will try to do what they can about it.

His servant shrugged at the doorway with tired eyes red from a life of confusion, a sagging yellowed face, and gray eyes.

"Maximus…."

When he heard his name called, the servant shivered like cold wind blew in. He froze in silence, inhaling more stale air to fill his lungs to respond.

"Maximus!"

"Y—yes, Sir—Master! Yes, master? What is it, Master?"

"Bring The Creator."

The servant had no time to think about why the emperor would order him to do this. He only listened and executed on his orders as any good servant would. He was getting paid for this, kept safe and comfortable by the emperor. A servant was only as good as he was able to serve.

"Yes, Master. I will bring The Creator to you. It will be done."

He wondered about wine. The king before him always drank the purple elixir, and it seemed to make him happier in times of trouble when he swigged from the golden goblet. Maybe he could try it.

"And make haste, *please*. Hurry and bring me The Creator!"

"Wha—what? I'm sorry, Master; what was that?"

"I said, 'hurry up!'"

The Creator would come and enter the storm of The Emperor's mind. An angry tempest stirred and would strike the next simple victim on a stage much larger than those that walked it.

Chapter 13

A King Enlightens A King

A young tan man with eyes full of fear looked up at his father. The figure stood tall above him, casting a shadow over the young man. He shivered in the cold of the dark.

"Father, may I ask you something?"

"Of course, my son."

"Erm... why were you so... why were you so intent on building something that would last for a while... only to be toppled over time by sun, wind, and sand? Why would you go through so much trouble in protecting an empire, knowing full well that nothing can last forever with the elements of change?"

"Hmm. Well, Oro, I continued the great kingdom that I inherited... to make it last as long as it could. To feed my people—my many seeds."

But the son didn't get the hint. He needed answers. "And why that? Was it for your people in particular? Or humanity in general?"

Hissing-red angry eyes. A grunt and a yell. A cry like a lone animal alone in the cold. Dark night with no hope and only the energy to hurt. His father punched a glass window and shattered the glass, crashing the walls with an angry sound. The red blood of the once-great king stained the white floors, walls, and couches of the place as it poured from his broken hand. Still, in the giant mansion, his drops of crimson life looked like gigantic waves looming over the spotless palace. Menizak's stains soaked even the marble that stood below them both.

Oro widened his eyes. "Father, do you need help with tha—"

"Shut up! Just be quiet, Oro. This is blood you've never bled, and *I'd bleed it again for a thousand years* if I could! And I'd bleed... for all time's sake until I leave forever. But the earth is nothing to me. I built things that will never leave!" He smeared his gushing-red hand all over his face and forehead so the blood soaked his red eyes and ran into his mouth, soaking his lips. His crazed face revealed two eyes that sang wide with a craven joy, such a spirited chorus of laughing voices screeching as he tried to separate body from soul. Maroon soaked into his skin like the drops of the first red-dead leaves to fall in autumn. All those crimson tears formed a leather dark that dripped with death and ecstatic life. He laughed and he cried as his son watched in total silence and stillness. *Was he behaving like a king? What did that even mean? What was a king but just a man who commanded others to call him thus?*

"Father... I don't understand."

Menizak III stood up and breathed heavily, chest heaving with deep and desperate sighs. His eyes of rotting steel were so bright and still ravenous for more blood. His hand and face and robes ran red and smelled of metallic rusted. The crimson kept running, coursing, engulfing the shards of glass stuck in his shaking hand. But no wind came in through the window. Blood spurted on the ground. Silent. White stained to red.

Oro's tender feeling for his father fled from him as he watched the madman grind his teeth and look on with yellow eyes. *Father...* Oro thought. *This man, person.... This 'thing' brought me into this world. He raised me and tried his best to love me. And now that love seems to be from someone else, not my father any longer. I behold now 'The King of Idaza.' His crown made him something I never wanted to be. I look so young and innocent in the reflection of his gold crown.*

Oro's quivering lips failed to make a sound. The wine-red blood all over the animal and the room made his tense body crave a drink—something to calm the sharpness of his sights and tame the wild image of a man he used to love, but no longer recognized. That man turned into some savage beast, some inhuman monster that hated humans, and therefore became less of his own. The same type of person he swore to destroy on his many campaigns far and wide. He looked around and saw nothing, hearing only the echoes of his father's cries. It all seemed to shrink as he looked back on a life lived in fear. He let slip what little he had, and now the afterlife removed the veil of his sanity for what the world really was: mad men doing things only for pleasure, out of anger. Bound by silver shackles, sunken in goblets of gold, his life was a path of wrong choices.

But the boy! *The boy. Oh, what does this all really mean? Is he the only hope for a fallen kingdom? But why would I care for a kingdom built by a man like this? By a man like me? By a man like my grandfather? Or his before him? Warlords and drunks and madmen? They only wanted power! No virtue. No rest. No righteousness or peace. That is why I failed. I was different from them, and whether or not the gods wanted me to be so or if they care for a fallen creature like me or if they even exist at all, I can accept that. I can accept all of it. No, I say yes to life*!

Oro sat still as his father continued to seethe and foam at the mouth. The older king smeared his blood all over, marking the walls and windows in crimson figurines. His eyes died long ago, and Oro thought he died alongside this old man.

But feeling his father's love quickly melt into madness made him think of the few good times—the handful of good feelings—that he felt before this *Purgatorio*. But he accepted it all the same. The young second-hand prince turned into the old gray king, becoming much like his father, facing him in the same circle of life that made him who he was, whether he liked it or not. His thoughts and wishes meant nothing, and the throne he sat on was only made of velvet and wood. Velvet could be ripped, and wood could be burned. He sat atop the throne as his father withered away, as he lay dying. And what all the death and loss meant to Oro's simple mind soon meant little, as he accepted the madness, smirked at the chaos, and looked his bleeding father in the eyes. It was a quick transformation, but he took it all in stride as the pain became a flame. He reached for the burning candle on the table in front of his father. His eyes went dark and stolid as the older man grated his teeth and sliced more of his skin—his neck, his chest, his hands, and his face.

Oro had never thought about much, and he did even less. But this feast of the senses would only last so long yet would ring out in the endless soul of the pudgy royal who never could get quite what he wanted.

King Oro, with the candle in hand, lit the pyre that was his bleeding, seething father with dead eyes and only an otherworldly will to self-destruct and destroy—as humans so naturally do. He was just like any other human. He'd never seen his father bleed before. He'd never seen his father prepare for anything but war. He was not a priest or a holy man. He was a warrior-king. He fought and fought more until he ruled more. That was the Menizak way. But Oro wanted to burn what was left of the shambles of the family—*his family*. He accepted the excellence with the petulance. He didn't hate his bloodline's big-chested dominance. He didn't hate the waves of the world, undulating with the curves of history. The key to Oro's salvation was this: he didn't hate a thing yet knew it needed to end. And he ended it all—the iron rule of The Menizaks imposing their will over others, extracting everything they could from the people they conquered. But even if that was the natural order of things, he didn't anger at his own bloodline, as he thought it was just another part of humanity—something flawed and beautiful and disgusting, just like him, just like the rest of us. So Oro just accepted it. He saw it all simply. Through his childish eyes, he returned to the pain of unbelonging, being misplaced in a world where everyone seemed to fit in fine. And he thought how in all that suffering there may have been joy and beauty, and how none of it made sense to him, but it didn't have to.

Humans made tools to hurt and help. Humans never made fire—they only discovered it.

I'm just like him; I'm just like my father, Oro thought.

"I'm just like you, Father."

His heart and mind took in a deep and sweet medicine just like the flame in his hand drew in air to live and grow.

His father never ran or retaliated, but just stood there as the unquenchable flame from the candle ate at his robe. The blaze of running orange grew more fearsome, clinging to his robes and spreading quickly as smoke sizzled the air. The mighty King Menizak III only stood there, being cleansed by the bite of the flame from head to toe.

The blaze caught on slow but soon burned brightly, breathing air, eating flesh, and only coughing dark black smoke in its wake. The fire didn't waver; it just did its deed until Oro could only recognize his father by his eyes as he began to seethe and writhe. Withering and then melting into a smoking pile of wiggling flesh. He shrieked in agony and threw himself on the ground, on the couches, and on the table, lighting it all ablaze as he yelled. He cried, but his tears would never be enough to quench the hungry flame.

But Oro didn't shiver at the sight. He didn't gasp or run away. He accepted the fate of his father just as he came to peace with his own. And all those people he ruled over lived by the projections of fire but never got so close as to be consumed by it.

Oro's mind went dangerously wild. *But power is raw and real—not in ruling, killing, or commanding—in accepting the sifting sands and the ever-changing tides of life. Of Existence. Of Earth and the pain that life holds. I smiled and cried so, and for so many years I suffered in wine and purple tears that stung my eyes, but that only meant much to me—no one else seemed to care. But... that's okay. In an indifferent world, it's okay. It's all okay.*

Oro watched with a frown as the flames consumed his father, growing larger to fill the room with smoke, growing brighter to make way for shadows that danced with death, pain, and purpose. But it wasn't the purpose that the younger king cared about. In fact, he couldn't care less about the purpose of the burning, why he was there, or the pain he caused himself and others. Maybe this was selfish. Maybe this was trite and childish by Oro, a man-child always running from his problems. But he grew numb to the pain and the lies and the cold deceit of the world and its tricks. He accepted them callously and watched his bloodline burn for the final time. The scorching flames hurt and choked Oro's throat and reddened his eyes. It would be the last time those eyes shed tears soaked in the soot of his father's ashes.

He heard all of his father's calls for help. He listened closely to every scream and agonized word of that 'once great man.' His father was not only a permanent fixture of his memory, but a lasting image of his bold, stoic face hung around so many paintings and marble busts around the haunting palace he called home his whole life.

But the pain of the flame cleansed all that. The light of the blaze extinguished all of Oro's fear for the place he was in now. The melting horror of a killed king kept burning and singing the carpets as the all-white house turned to a home for horrors.

And yet, Oro smirked at the violence and the suffering for what he hoped would be the last time.

He waited. He stood as still as time itself, watching his father's essence evaporate into the air. Through the broken window, a burst of wind swept the stench away forever. The younger son listened to the shrieks soften into silent moans. The whole house reeked of burnt flesh. Black smoke filled the room.

Soon, the rage of the fire was the only thing heard before The Last Menizak of the great bloodline was smothered into ash and raw skin. His gaping jaw showed white-clean teeth that mimicked the brightness of the still-living eyes of the old gray king.

Through the searing scream of the flame, a single whisper could be heard. The voice was unmistakable— although garbled and cracked, the voice of a broken man shone through the black smoke.

"I always wanted to... help."

"Me too, Father."

The ceiling caved in from above, the walls collapsed in dense dust while smoke stifled the breath of them both as the burned man lay dead in a smoldering pile, while Oro slowly drifted into a black oblivion as his whole body convulsed into silence for eternity.

No more words were necessary. No more words were needed.

No matter how brightly the heart of a warrior burned, it was always the flames to fear.

It would always be the flames to fear, for humans never invented fire but discovered it, found it, and never truly recovered its full purpose ever, not even until this scientific day. But the flame would soon cleanse a whole lot of souls, a sum of flesh unspoken. Maybe it'd be painful up close to being burned by the fire. But from far away, it was a beautiful spectacle of lights and creation and death and vision and sound and springtime red that made the people smile.

Smile. And if you can't smile in the smoke of the flame, then succeed in the soot as it sprays in the air. Walk through it. Cough and cripple; bow down to the fangs of the flame. Humans were blessed with that great gift, but what's better—the gift or the curse? The best way to celebrate death is with a birth.

Chapter 14

Scared Children Never Grow Up

But Mikalla was not brave, just a scared child with stupid courage. He thought about his son, whom he left above earth. Visions of Coyote's face were all he saw as he fell; spears dug into his tender torso as he fell hundreds of feet, leaving that boy forever alone in an uncaring world. He thought about his own seed he left above the earth as he sank into its dirt forever.

He sobbed.

"I miss him, Jani. I miss him so much."

Her grip held tighter on the knife. She seethed. Clench of the jaw, bob of the throat. Her tongue swirled. "He's away now. We no longer exist," she said with teeth tightened.

"Can you tell him I love him?"

"I can't. But... I think he already knows." She trailed off and stared long into a distance unknown. She turned away into the air and across the stars. Her green, emerald eyes became mossy chasms empty. She never wanted to be there, and it was her weak and emotional husband that got her there. They were both dead and gone, and it was his fault.

It's all his fault. But Coyote really did love him.... And that little boy loved his father for who he was. Did he love me, though? Did he ever? Does he now? Jani thought.

Mikalla continued to cry. "I never wanted this."

"Well, *I* never wanted any of this."

"I think we want the same things, Jani." Mikalla fixed his sharp red eyes on the dagger his wife gripped— in all its ornaments and powerful symbols of a family's deep rich history as a people used to power and maintaining their grasp by knife or by handshake. Jani's lineage was a timeless story told through that silver dagger, enriched with beauty and fine detail but deadly all the same. It would be so fitting for the family that failed Jani and cast her aside as one of many children who wanted to enjoy the sweet, ripe fruits their legacy yielded to destroy Mikalla, The Last Conjurer. Though Jani resented her husband and made sure he knew it at every turn of a word, she hated herself more than him. Ever since she was a child, she was taught and fed the belief daily that she was lesser, and all she wanted to be was *more*.

There is no light without dark, but the woman's eyes have seen so little light since she was a bruised and battered child, abandoned in a palace trimmed with gold and marble spires.

"I ca—I *won't* kill you." She lowered the knife with a shaking hand.

"And why not?"

"Because I've never killed before. And... I wouldn't kill you."

"But I've already been killed, Jani. I've held the highest position in the land and had the privilege of performing in the best way, the way anyone who has ever lived would love to perform for their livelihood—*authentically*. The waves I've made will affect generations to come…. And then what? What do the stories matter? What does the sharpness of my pen mean if we both stand here right now, betrayed by those close to us, and dishonest with ourselves? I don't have all the answers, Jani, and so that's why I explore the dark of the unknown with reckless abandon," Mikalla said, smiling, "with childlike *wonder* and *amaze*ment. There's no thing in life as great as *not* knowing. You can continue to know in the dark. You can be the light for others."

Jani looked at the ground. Her face was flush and sunken-pale. "So what's your point?"

"That I do know some things. That I may not know what *love* is or even be able to define the outermost bounds of what it means to love someone, but *do* I know that I love you. I know simply that I cannot ask for more, or, at least, it would be stupid to do so—to regret things that have already happened and to despise life because of some suffering in the past. I know we made someone good. I know we *did* a lot of good... *together*, Jani. We did it all together." Mikalla smiled. "And with no doubt, you may not think that you care, but I know deep down you'd always wanted to feel useful and to feel loved. Not in general, Jani, bu—"

"And your point! *What's your point*? Get to it. Oh, *Mikalla*, get to it! You always do this and never make your point! Your stories go on and on and on, and you never really say what it is—what it *means*! What are you saying, Mikalla?"

"I want you to feel loved right now. I want you to feel useful right now. I want you, Jani, to feel powerful right now. Because you're all those things. I know that nothing's certain, and though I've impacted countless imaginations all throughout the world, it doesn't mean I can impact yours. But I'd like to. I'd *love* to. I'd really...." And through tears, Mikalla set a final oath. He choked out his chosen words through a sore throat and an empty chest. "And I've just wanted, in my own vain pursuits of glory and being loved—being *great*... to *everyone*—to also bring fire to the people. That flame has warmed those who watch its shadows, and eruptions of burning pain for those who embrace it. But I've never wished for anyone, anywhere, to have a painless existence. I've never wished for blood not to be shed or for there to be no blood. And so they can suffer as I have, and for that I'd be no different from them. But you've always been the one I've most wanted—possibly the only one—who I've wanted nothing but to have comfort and warmth." Mikalla turned harsh in his next words with heavy breath and a beating heart that wore weary in his chest. He looked at the same weak, lonesome spot on the ground that Jani stared at, and he stared too. It wasn't some dark abyss, but just a piece of white marble floor. "I... know what you've done. I know what you've thought. I saw it before the spears ever pierced me so ruthlessly. And I can't forgive you because I haven't yet figured out what forgiveness truly is. But I don't care. I love you. I don't have to know love to know that."

"And... so what, Mikalla?" Jani's eyes streamed with tears at the storyteller's tale, guarding her fearsome gray heart against his wanton, wandering words.

"So I want you to *feel* loved. Because I've loved you always and I still do. Because... I could drown in a sea of applause, but without you, it'd still just be drowning."

Jani didn't smile at this but shrugged and kept her sight fixed on the floor. Her red eyes welled up with tears too. What more could she gain in a room with only one man? What more secrets were there with only one heart present, which she'd already explored to its deepest depth? She gained the world, but after some death, violence, and decay, she could only stare at the ground, which made her. It was a shiny floor, the type she was used to walking on.

"I have nothing to gain. Nothing to lose. Only a malicious and awful deed done right behind my back by people I cannot control put me here. In this position. With you again."

The once-great, now-dead storyteller responded in the only way he knew how. It wasn't enough to have an ear lent to him. He needed to own it, along with the eyes and the minds of those around him. "Then listen to me, Jani…."

"You have nothing left to say. Your stage is rubble. Your audience has gone on without you, Mikalla. Your flames died long ago. You preach to no one."

"No one but you."

It was then that Jani felt a twinge, a tweak in the rhythm of her chest that twisted shortly. She realized that maybe, maybe, Mikalla's audience could have included her all along.

Possibly, I was the one who he wanted to influence and the only one who wouldn't fit under the spell of his fictional tales of times lost and past. He still seems like such a boy, even now after all these years. He's a little pathetic and a lot childish.

"And so, Jani, I only have *one person* left in my audience, which was once millions. I have *one story* left from a mind once littered with peril and beauty. I'm nearly exhausted from all that I've ever wanted... except for one last story."

"And what story is that?"

"I love you. I loved you then, and I will love you until there is no will left; that's my story. I've always respected you and felt for you. Anytime you hurt, I hurt twice. Every time you fell, it felt like I tumbled deeper." Mikalla looked away as if to fantasize about a time long passed. Maybe that time had passed and that moment left. "Your smile... your *everything*. You *are* everything."

Jani's gaze froze into a trance. Her eyes glazed over in stillness and sadness. She now regretted every word, and it was not the words she said that hurt, but the loathing that burned her insides. Words themselves meant nothing to her, only the things they could bring. And now her words could win her little, and so it all felt closed and dark in her empty eyes. All felt dark and unwanted—every sight and sound, memory, and moment that surfaced gave her pause.

But it was pain—deep and abiding suffering—that bore the true fruit of man. Jani's pain was no different, as it felt like the shedding of her raw skin, clenching, then falling off her bones to make room for flesh anew. This was her metamorphosis—why she was there, why Mikalla was there, both picked by one another, needing the other to perform so mightily as to fit in the other's soul. She thought of that little girl she once knew; it was herself, the little trampled girl overshadowed by all her older siblings, none caring for the girl who just wanted an embrace, but that embrace came too late.

Or maybe none of it was ever meant to be, and it was an awful mess from the start. Maybe the meaning Mikalla had always strove for was in vain after all. What would be the beauty in that? Where was the triumphant tale to be told about a vain attempt his whole life, running a fool's errand and pouring his soul into a cracked vase, leaking all he gave into the ground until the man had nothing left but damp dirt to stare into?

Is there any beauty? We would have to see. Maybe we'd have to find beauty on our own. Maybe what we held dear was really dear, and that which made us twist and turn at night was evil.

Maybe our bodies really did speak the truth, and listening to the screech of our ancestors from beyond the grave could help us live better in our present moments. But it stayed so hard to keep a keen ear to the echoes of the past. That was the problem.

Mikalla spit on the spotless floor.

Chapter 15

A Baby Stolen By The State Again

"Miss, we will offer you a handsome price if it comes out a boy."

"What if it's a girl?"

"Then pain."

"I can't part with him. Even if it's a boy, I couldn't ever leave this. He would need me." The woman sobbed. She had sparse black hair on top of a pink, sweaty face of tears and fearful eyes. She came from a low class of people where women, objects, beasts, men, and tools were all meant to be used by rich people. She and her child were just tools to make money for those that already had it—women, beasts, dirt; they were all the same, just a commodity or another coin for the class that controlled them. But she thought of her child's future—that's all she could think of. Maybe it could even grow to live and walk on its own.

"You may want to... *reconsider*." The hairy man cleared his throat and shoved his garment aside, revealing a dirty dagger on his belt. "There may be pain for you, Miss. I get that. But I think you'll understand soon enough about your—"

"About my what?" The woman was in labor and struggled to speak. Every word was strained, and every movement hurt worse than her shriveling heart. She sweated and strived and pushed in pure loneliness, abandoned by all those who cared, swarmed by men with knives that lurked only for profit. She felt like she was going to die. How could someone bringing new life into the world regret being born? The woman in labor worked harder and pained more than the profiteering pirates that swarmed her. They were like ghouls with no souls, and she felt the pain and the ecstasy of a new soul entering the world, seeing its tiny pinhead for the first time.

"Your *situation*." The man's dirty dagger shone like a pearl in the dark. Neither the pregnant woman nor the bearded man could have seen a thing if not for the light of the flickering flame in between them. It lit the old leather walls of the widow's shabby hut a bright orange, heating their faces all sweating. It was all perfectly silent then. Not even the tiny orange flame whispered. They both thought about the threat of the rusty knife's slick edge. The woman thought about her son-to-be.

My life is not worth as much as his. He's the future. He's... my child... a light cast unto the world, and whatever gave him life finally made me happy to die. He's my hope. He's my life. He's my horizon. Maybe this little thing could bring light to more than just me once he grows. The woman sobbed. Sobbed. *I only want him to grow old and happy with a child of his own. This may be his best chance at being happy.*

They've cornered me in a dark place. They've swindled me out of what little life I had left and given me no chance... and yet they give him a chance. They give this baby boy—and I do hope it's a boy—a value for some reason. I don't believe it's their kindness, but something from the gods that has brought us this far. I'm alive, for a bit... and with any blessing from the gods above, my son may live much longer than me. He may even do something that topples the people that have held his bloodline down for so, so long.... So many generations of suffering. Maybe by the gods or my own delusion, they believe this little unborn blob may be a leader. A legend. A predator finally born.... He may finally be something more than a slave or a young death that mattered to no one. Please, gods, let this be a boy, and let this boy be the man he wants to be.

Maybe the suffering of her whole ancestry was bred for one single chance at a whiff of power, a slim chance to snatch influence and change and free so many peasant minds and enslaved bloodlines. Her mother shamed her for having this child with some unnamed man that ran away without honor; her grandmother would never approve, but yet they all came from lives of bondage and servitude. *Maybe this boy could be different. Maybe this boy could break our long line of bondage.* She shed many tears for many reasons.

The mother cried during the birth of her child. After the birth of her child. She looked into its eyes. Her tears soaked her sallow cheeks in awe. It was a new being, a new birth on an earth that churned death like the most vicious machine.

"It's a boy," one of the men said.

She sobbed louder, running out of tears to cry.

She didn't have a choice.

The baby boy never had a choice. He entered a cruel world where only masters and slaves existed. His mom could barely breathe as the light of the orange flame dimmed. She saw the void creeping in on her vision, everything growing darker. No stars were in her sky.

If there were always going to be owners, then even they may not have had a choice to buy the boy and separate the mother from the only joy she had left. The woman reasoned that this was how the world worked, and they didn't have choice, much like she didn't have one then. When she gave that boy away, when the last little pink pride was pried from her wiry arms by the bearded man and his associates, they promised nothing and said nothing—for she had nothing left to give. They just took it.

"He's in our custody now. I hope you get well."

Fluids leaked all over the bed. Streams ran down her face and body. She heaved, feeling like life was closing the door on her. She stopped fighting the stress and pain and just lay there speechless, out of breath and out of ways to think. Her body began to quit on her, organs slowing, heart shrinking, eyes going darker into the future of a great bleak nothing.

The baby cried, and the mother looked at the man with tired eyes and a gaping mouth. She only had the strength to whisper one final note. "Please take care of him. Let… him grow."

"We will." The men stood around her and nodded.

With her final breath, she whimpered out a request. She was promised compensation for her firstborn son. Even on her deathbed as she birthed her only child, she thought about gold coins. "When will I get my payment?"

His mustache curled in a smirk. "The question is, for me, how will you take the payment from us? You gave up the only thing worth anything, and now you are back to the dirt from which you came. Are you really going to fight spears with your dirt and naked arms?" He laughed as a coy smile formed on his lips, looking around to his men, who also chuckled around the crying newborn. "You now have nothing again. And with nothing, you can get nothing, *peasant*." He spit on the ground before signaling his guards to leave with him through the opening in the walls of the shanty hut.

"Mercy... please... I beg of you. *Please*.... I cannot eat." She shivered in the orange flicker of the flame, too little to warm anything, only a candle's worth of light. She couldn't cry and could barely speak, yet she forced words out of her throat in anguish over the coming cold night. The dark night would soon be her only blanket and only companion, as it had for so long before then. She whispered into the world as if no one could hear her soft words. "Take care"

"What was that, you say?"

"Take care of... him."

"Oh, he'll be well looked after." The man's orange face went dark once he grabbed the tiny flame and turned the flicker to a sad gray wisp. No more shadows danced in the hut, as the lone woman could only hear the men scurrying out of her hut with her son captive.

Her hands were so full of new life, young promise, and unbound potential just moments ago. And now she held nothing, looked at nothing, and listened to footsteps trample away from her into the night. The woman felt cold and clammy as sweat poured from her skin and tears ballooned and popped from her face. She was left alone again—something taken, nothing given back.

She clung to the idea of hope—the *hope* that one day she may see her son again, healthy and thriving and freed from bondage, free to live his days as he pleased, even when trials came his way. But the tears told her another story; her tears told the truth: she would never see him another time, and she may never love anything like that small pink child again.

Maybe she would become a psychotic person. How could that mother adjust again to normal society after everyone and everything leaves her like a fallen autumn leaf? There were no mental hospitals in Idaza, so she just cried.

And she cried. She cried in the dark with no child left and no one to protect the vulnerable woman who was pink in the face from the pain. Her only hope was new life—not her own, but the one that passed through her from somewhere else.

Maybe that baby boy would be free one day. But we all know he would be.

Those with freedom have the funny urge to enslave as many others as they can. They didn't even give that boy a name, and his mother didn't have the strength to think of one. Just another nameless orphan now.

After many gasps in the dark, she had no more tears to cry as her eyes went dry and her vision got blurry. The woman finally lay in rest. Her tears purely purged all of her hatred and angst, her sorrow and self-pity, and all those things that make us want to end our lives, wish we were never born, and wish for some heaven to save us after we see the silver curtain eclipse our eyes for one final time. She died.

More sweat to quench the dirt. There would be more to come, as no story ever ended with the death of the parent but the birth of the child. This story was far from over.

Chapter 16

The Savage Awakens

Coyote rushed breaths, huffing with his face in his arms. Dry cheeks dirtied on the filth of his sleeves. His feet trembled on the ground, shaking the table he laid his head on. He groaned like a dog, quivering legs, running in place, sitting, wanting to yell until his face went red and all his blood vessels popped But he was still. He just sat and grunted to himself, tensing every muscle like a lit fuse ready to explode. All the questions he asked had already been answered. He hunched in his chair like some beast in agony, gashing its teeth in slobber. Face shrouded. Fangs hidden. His memory was unclear. He wanted to fight or harm or watch something in as much pain as him, fantasizing about only quick-easy violence.

His heart held onto things he could never grasp; he reached for the wind and tried to capture the sun.

He entertained Death. But there was more to care for—still maybe a small, bright glimmer to keep his will to stay alive for one last, explosive performance. What was an artist, a worker, or a person without their performance? Even an emperor had to perform. Coyote felt like he could never perform like those great ones of the past or all those inevitable generations to come.

A pebble that looked up toward great trees that towered over him.

You're no different than an emperor. You suffer more than you hope and always achieve more than you would think.

It was all a pit crawling with two-legged beasts; the warm-hearted humans froze by the frigid blood of their own friends. Don't forget that you're a beast who would kill or be killed to survive. You're just a tall animal on two legs who could run for a while if you're fit for it.

The only hope is that you grasp hope tightly and take the life you're given for everything it's worth, and it's worth more than anything could replace.

***

Caring, cold, stupid, or great, Coyote was the one who was deemed the young emperor, and no noble person seemed to care about his absent mind. He ate the fruits of many generations before him who fought for his right to lounge and be sad and frail. He couldn't even enjoy the fruits of their bloodshed.

The servant entered the hallway and called his master. But the servant was quietly smart—as any good servant was—to maneuver around political connections and interests. Every servant risked serving the wrong master. But this servant took his gamble in serving the young scraggly man with the empire in his palm. He'd rather just listen to the orders and take his chances, earning the trust of the only person who could save or make his life—a bearded boy named Coyote.

But Coyote finally gave way to a new thirst for cleanliness. Something electrified the boy; some strike of lightning shot through his spine and widened his eyes. His tired groans grew to anxious howls. The cold echoes of Coyote's screech chilled the ears of the nobility. It was as if the whole empire froze for a moment.

Coyote shot up to shave his beard. He grabbed his bloody razor and shed his whiskers and all the mistakes of his parents' past—the hair of old past suffering, cleansing his face, and washing it with the clean water of a king. It washed away the blemishes of a dirty face, a forest of dark memories grown from hurtful memories long past. He didn't notice that his pile of hair clogged the drain.

His clean-cut face revealed deep creases of worry over the few years he walked the earth. He looked in the mirror anew, a fresh face ripe for new design, ready to shape the world in his own hands. He took the razor once more and slowly sliced a notch at the tips of both his cheeks. He made a couple slits in his eyebrows, so his face was the color of a hot red flame.

With every cut, he was less himself and more of the world. Closer to death, yet feeling manic with green life, electrified by the chance of a new day and all its goodness. He laughed in the mirror at his thoughts, his bloody, disfigured face, and his dark mind lit by the visions of flames everywhere.

The nobles put up with the emperor because he didn't bother him, and his letters to the people kept everything in its proper place, frozen in time. But Coyote cackled at the idea of ice. Ice would melt and thaw with the simplest switch. Life made the young man fearless; loss made his losses hurt less, numb from the thorns and prickly thickets. He feared nothing in the face of the changing wind and the constant tides, and so he needed The Creator, who he called upon just minutes before he wailed like a monster from the deep that just arose, finally awoken to all the ills. He felt for his people and their lives. Every droplet of blood that dripped from his jaw onto the floor made him more of the earth he formed from. His yellow fangs looked white against his stark crimson skin. His eyes were bloodshot from staying awake even as God's night tried to tuck him in. He smiled and laughed some more. Some more blood dripped and ran and formed a mask. He grinned in the mirror one last time at a monster he couldn't recognize. He loved the monster. He loved the fangs and the yellowed teeth stained with drips of maroon drops. He liked the animal he saw. For once, he liked what he saw in the mirror because he couldn't quite make who or what it was.

Maybe the rich and spoiled noble people had wives they cared about, husbands they kissed by candlelight, and children they embraced after a long day of work. But they all had to be sacrificed to the fire. Maybe they would scream their human screams. But the screeches of anguish were just music to the monster in the mirror.

He wrote letters in the dark so long to let his people into the light. He thought once more of that little flame that always sat by his side like a loyal dog on dark nights. It wasn't until he put on his ragged hood and ventured into the commons to watch that one mother push away her child into the woods to give him the satisfaction he needed in order to secure his spot as still the rightful Conjurer of the land. He had no dissidents, no one that oppressed him that still lived. And yet his eyes glinted a killing streak to come. More blood dripped down. He cut himself more. He couldn't feel the pain.

And then the person he needed greeted him in his own lone childhood home at long last after only minutes of waiting for him.

"My Great Emperor, I am here to serve you and bless you in whatever way you deem best to use my services.... And I'm proud to be at your service, Your Highness."

These were the exact words an emperor yearned to hear after a life of long misery. His letters to his people he always doubted, no matter how strongly he watched with his own eyes how his words affected his people in a good way—his own... *good way*. He saw flames in his eyes.

"I'll be right out."

"What was that, Sir?"

"I said, 'I'll be right out!'"

And he continued to etch his will onto the page. And he continued to spill his own red blood deep in the crevices of being and blank space. He searched the page with his own rage, wanting to numb the feelings he knew he never could. While he wrote and published his letters for the masses, the world came to a halt.

But the sun always rose again against his will. He could command the strongest beings that rose from the dirt, but not dirt itself; he couldn't command the earth he stood on or the sky he saw above. But it was that helplessness that fueled his pen and lit the flame of his angst; in a world so unkind, how could he refrain from returning the favor of all the wretched evil he watched since a child? For he was just a boy for long but soon became a man, only changing in his view of the world: that it was a harsh place that turned movement into menace. The only thing he learned in his life was that it was a harsh thing to live. For the mighty hand of suffering could lend help toward a greater being.

Life made people this way. *All those beautiful humans hurt from loss were just like me. They were scarred from lies as soon as they could listen, stolen from as soon as they got something. Robbed. Extorted. Tortured. Exploited....*

But someone powerful killed his father, and he could never forgive that. Even a monster had loyalty and love. And now he summoned The Creator to do some of the same that had been done to him.

"He is here, Master."

"Alone? Is he alone?"

"He seems to be alone, Master."

"Well, make sure he comes alone! That's what I asked for."

"He is accompanied by no one, Your Highness. He is alone."

Coyote smirked at the dusty, dark walls of his room. With letters and simple words, Coyote reduced the past to dust. "Well, then, good: bring him up."

"What was that?"

"Bring him up! Now, please!"

Coyote stepped out of the dark into the line of light.

"I'm here, Your Highness…."

"*Yes.* Yes! Yes? Come on up. Come up here!"

"I'll be right there."

"Maximus, leave us, please," Coyote said.

"Yes, Master."

"Maximus—"

"Yes?"

"I mean, leave us totally. Go away and don't come back until the sun yawns and dusk sets in. I want total solitude with this most *honorable* man."

The servant widened his eyes. The emperor hated how he had to repeat himself as if his words didn't mean a thing.

"Is this understood?"

"Yes, Master. I will return as the blue sky turns to pink."

"What?"

"I will be back when the sun sets!"

"Good. Now, go. Now. I have a very esteemed guest here." He grinned at the high priest, who stood still and straight, perfectly postured with a subtle smile.

The servant bowed down and strode into the shadows. He chose to keep the emperor happy for the chance to live to see another day and keep his family fed and comfortable. After all, what was a man who didn't aim to please others?

The servant pretended not to see the emperor's sliced face. He chose to ignore his crazed eyes and blood-stained teeth.

Once they were left alone, Lupus bowed deeply in the presence of the more powerful person—as other powerful people often do.

Lupus the wolf was the last to survive his broken family. His distant father taught him well by never showing him affection. He was a high priest too. He learned his best tactics from his father, who never talked much, and so he only spoke when he had to. Ever since a boy, he flew high by the fraying tethers of a large, rich, broken-loveless family. The sunshine gleamed through spotless windows each day, but his childhood home was always cold, always alone among the busy halls.

He'd learned certain things along the way to his prominent position: patience, deceit, and *humility*. He grew up in an empty house full of people that paid little attention to him. Whenever his parents, siblings, or servants needed something from him, they just called his name. Lupus stopped longing for hugs and kind words when he was still young. He only hungered more with every rich feast his parents held. He became a wolf. Among sheep, he was excellent and dangerous. Among wolves, he *fit in*. That ability to wait in the shadows long enough for the right time to strike delivered the high priest to the peaks of power.

Lupus grew up in a traditional kingdom once ruled by his uncle, a mighty king that commanded whoever he pleased to do whatever he wanted, whenever he wanted it.

But Lupus knew from his spies that this emperor was nothing like any king who came before him. His spies reported that this man usually just sat in dark silence and wrote stories to the people of Idaza before going on long walks and drinking himself stupid. He read every letter of every message to try to get to know the emperor better. He had climbed so far and waited so long to be within a few warm breaths of Coyote, the pathetic little boy. That naïve child learned to trust Lupus from afar—after all, why would the emperor have any reason to fear such a holy man?

Right there, at the top of the staircase, and with no guards, Lupus could stab, punch, or brutalize the young man. But that would only create a power vacuum he would quickly get sucked into while more heads rolled. Coyote's life was both valuable and meaningless to Lupus—he needed the emperor to live so the nobles would stay content with full bellies. Without an emperor sitting safely at the top of the pile, they might get hungry for more scraps.

He didn't care for the man, but only the man's position and all the possessions and power he could siphon for himself like sweet nectar. He hoped to feel a full belly from the juice he would drain from the silly-lost-stupid young boy. He didn't comment on the fresh blood soaking Coyote's face, running rivers down his eyes, mouth, and jaw.

"My Gracious Emperor, what prompted you to summon me today? Are you, perhaps, working on anything new?"

"I have a few things I'm working on. I'm always working." Coyote chuckled, and his laugh tore up a storm inside his gut. The high priest laughed alongside him, even if it was forced and fake. They looked away from one another and chuckled more as their smiles faded.

Lupus tried his best to giggle, looking down at the cold marble floor. "I hope, My Lord, that what you're working on is something that will bring light to the people."

"Well, I feel as though... oh, I think there's not much more to... well, I've studied all the best before me…. There don't seem to be any more words. *Words*! It seems as though all the greatest stories have already been told,

Your Holiness. And yet, where would we be without words?" Coyote cackled as he slammed his fist onto the railing. "It's just that," Coyote said with a grin and cold, dead eyes. "These words don't come easy anymore, and I'm not sure…. I don't think…. I'm fine. The stories are fine! My stories are great and they help people! The art is fine. It's all fine. I'm fine. I hope you're fine, too. Well, I hope you're more than fine."

"Your Highness—"

"Just call me, 'Coyote.'"

Lupus inched closer to the young man. He could hear his throat clench, his tongue search and probe his tightened teeth and mouth, smell the sweat beading on his nose and in his hair. Lupus sensed a beating heart that caved and cracked every time it squeezed itself again. *This is a broken young man…. He's worse than I thought. What a pathetic, disgusting little kid wishing to be a man. What a travesty. This little piglet who thinks mud is good food. Disgusting. What a pathetic boy,* the high priest thought to himself.

"Coyote, my son, just tell me what vexes you. What is wrong? What could possibly be wrong for a man who has everything he could ever want?"

"A man who could have anything he wants could be happy. But I am not that. I can't have anything I want. It seems I am plagued with a sickness I cannot recover from."

"And so, My Glorious Emperor, what could possibly be the problem?"

Coyote shrugged and looked away. He thought of all the problems in his own small life. He'd seen the greatest sickness, the greatest loss, the deepest sadness, and the greatest reproach and betrayal from those he once called 'loved ones.' Thoughts of the worst times flashed through his mind as the most powerful man stood as a sad man. Misplaced. Misfit. Misunderstood and perfectly placed in a life that only took from helpless him. His face faded from grin to frown. He needed something he could never have again.

But he wouldn't tell Lupus any of his struggles—that wouldn't be the way of an emperor. "My problems are, let's say, both different and the same as all people. I have no sadness, unlike any of the common people. I have no problems that I am not equipped to handle. I will solve them on my own."

Lupus closed his eyes and nodded. He didn't wish to pry and upset the young man. "I pray to the gods that you be healed and find peace."

"I will never find peace. Peace is a capricious mistress that has no taste for me." Coyote laughed again, but this time, not from the heart or his chest, barely coughing up a chuckle, looking away from the priest.

"And so, what can I do for you, Coyote?" Lupus let the sun of the day warm his face and light his smile as he stood, shading the shorter man in a shroud of black.

Coyote's newly shaven face showed a craven look that begged for nothing. The young emperor's eyes said only things dark and desperate. He was young. He was handsome. He had power and wealth and did not have to work or want for much. And he was not happy and didn't like being asked what someone could do for him or how he was feeling. For what could he gain? For whom would he gain it? Himself?

He despised his own skin. He despised this damned life.

His kingdom? It abandoned him.

His late parents? They'd left him an orphan.

A girl? He figured she'd just leave when the time was right for her.

The family he didn't have? Friends? No. No, Coyote could never escape this pain—not even death could deliver him from the sorrow.

He felt that maybe, possibly, his last and only purpose was to wake every soul up from their slumber, for them all to realize that the pretty pictures on the walls illuminated by the flame were just pictures, just distractions from the true maze—that those walls would never end, and that their time should not be spent chasing fleeting moments of pleasure, but rather to escape the labyrinth that ensnared them all.

Sometimes, he didn't want to feel what he felt, but he never wanted to be numb. He trusted pain. It was distrust itself that brought him so much anguish. But his mind would not allow for such a trick. He knew—he knew all of it to be hopelessly true: the king of a labyrinth was still trapped just like his very subjects. He wanted the endlessness to end. He wanted them all to get out of the maze.

"I have a special deed I need done," Coyote whispered. He looked at the ground and stepped even closer to the high priest so they could be face-to-face.

"By the gods?"

"No. Not by them. By you." *They'll go to meet the gods soon enough*, Coyote thought to himself.

"And what is it that you'd like me to do?"

"I want you to order the sacrifice of every noble person who calls the palace of the late King Oro their home."

Lupus widened his eyes and blinked twice. He cleared his throat. "Sacrifice? To the gods?"

Coyote just shrugged. "Something like that. I don't really care. Just kill them."

Lupus smelled the stench of a crazed man—no longer just a lost cause or a coddled king, but a *threat*. "Are you sure you want this?"

Coyote leaned in and sharpened his tone, nearly pushing the high priest down the stairs with the force of his voice. The ruler could be a fox, a worm, and a lion— all three—but here, he felt the need to roar. "Never, ever question me! I call you 'The Creator,' and yet I don't call you 'Emperor!' Why is that?"

"Because I am not the emperor…. I am the High Priest of Idaza, just like my father before me."

"No, you're not an emperor or a king; you're not even a general! And I've lived through too many people getting betrayed by their own confidants, their own advisers, spouses, family, and…." Coyote widened his mouth, and for a flash, his eyes lit with a chance of bright insight. It was as if the void he saw so drowned for so long in black ink and grief was—if only for a moment—lit by a single point in time, played over throughout history, as if all the plants and people and sands of the earth had all seen the same things forever. He saw the circle of time from the outside—not just his life, but the infinite others who each clambered for meaning and purpose, like sapling sprouts searching for space to reach the height of great oaks in perilous forests of prey. No, human nature was not nice, and human nature was no different.

"Coyote, I can do your bidding as I'm told. I come from a long line of holy men who only seek to bless people while I convene with our guardians above."

"Yes, yes. And you must answer for them tonight." The young emperor whipped out a dagger from inside his ragged robes and swiped at the high priest. The small blade first tore a vein in Lupus' arm before he could defend himself. Blood spurted on the floor, on his robes, and on his face. And Coyote kept swiping and stabbing at the Lupus with unending ferocity, replaying every time in his life where he felt cornered and angry for it. The supposed gods that Lupus summoned so often couldn't protect him now, as they have never protected Coyote in the past. He swung the dagger with a tight grip and no precision, with the only aim being to draw enough blood to end the life of the man known as 'The Creator.'

Lupus, the bigger and stronger of the two, unarmed, tried to block every attack with his arm while swimming through to tackle Coyote. Lupus bled from more gashes as burgundy blood pooled onto the white marble floors. He yelled with no one to hear him—and in that way, he was like Coyote had been his entire life.

They both struggled and grunted and screeched. Lupus continued to bleed but ignored his wounds and thought about what he could do to survive. The emperor had already made up his capricious mind—there would be little to stop his childish whims from going and trying to kill the high priest. Therefore, it was Lupus who needed to kill the other man, despite his many cuts on his way to lunging finally—leaving his neck exposed to the knife—at the legs of Coyote. Lupus dove and wrapped his arms around his assailant. Coyote swung the knife like a hammer down to Lupus' head. It drove for the priest, homing in on his skull, its sharpest edge ending at a lethal point that's only purpose was to penetrate the high priests' brain matter.

Silver flashed. Lupus yelled. And Coyote was taken and tackled, so the knife that missed his head so loudly tumbled to the floor beside both men. Lupus scrambled, caught off guard and swinging his fists like hammers and his nails like claws on Coyote's skin. He had to kill the most powerful person in the nation—only to save himself. He had no time to think about the consequences of taking the young emperor's life. On the ground getting punched and bitten and struggling for his life, there were no gods here. Only flashes of red and black, shadows turning over and wrestling, scrambling in a mad pace for the dagger—that silver dagger.

Maybe the man's fists would be enough. He had to do something—and Lupus didn't think, but he acted the only way his body allowed him to. Mounted atop the smaller man, he unleashed an unholy barrage of fists. He punched and punched, looking for the dagger that was somewhere on the ground. His knuckles turned red, cut by Coyote's teeth. He did not feel anything. Claws dug into his sides. Maybe teeth. Knuckles. Elbows and vicious kicks turned vision fuzzy. Splotches of red seeped through the robes of the two men. It felt fast while time went slow. There wouldn't be a winner in bloodshed, but the loser would pay the ultimate price. But their bodies would not let up. No, they were locked in the ultimate game.

The emperor escaped the hold and slipped away. Lupus was still stunned and tried to catch his breath. The high priest felt a shooting pain in his groin. He felt his eyes sting and fill with red. They squirmed like worms at the top of the stairs.

The right side of Lupus' face shriveled to a reddened patch that concealed a swath of his vision that also hid the fist of Coyote, striking again that same eye furiously. Lupus could only see from his left eye a baring grin of grit teeth by a mad and lost man—someone who never considered for one second what he could lose or feel by killing a man because he'd already done it all. His eyes—the eyes of the younger, smaller, weaker man—still spoke of wisdom. And then another claw dug into his eye, scything its softness, and popping its white shell. The fight turned loud as Lupus screeched blindly. With both eyes closed, he could hear and feel the thumping knock of a bone break against his wild hammering fists. It was a rib. Coyote yelped as well, and then, broken and battered again and again, Lupus's blind punches hit the hard floor, breaking nothing except for the tops of his own knuckles.

Twisted. Blind and vile. Spit. Seething lips sputtered a sigh of agony as many teeth lay on the ground beside both men. Lupus looked around with blurry eyes, hearing Coyote stand up but not being able to see him. He didn't have the strength to twist his head. It even hurt the priest to blink.

Lupus lay on the ground. He wanted to shout but could only utter a weeping gasp as tears mixed with blood. His frantic feelings slowly melted into serenity. His hearing deadened as if his ears were plugged. The last thing he heard felt like a far-off whisper from the emperor that stood above him. "There will be blood."

The priest's limp body stuttered and stopped. Stuttered and stopped again, shivering like the legs of a dying cockroach. His vision went blood-black. And in his darkest moment, the high priest did not call out to the gods. Those mythical figments of his imagination were not even a thought, and not one of them reached out to save him as he lay dying like a bug. Maybe he would meet them. Maybe they would all be there to greet him at the great gates beyond. That was only a passing possibility; what was certain was that he would die on the cold marble floor in a helpless heap as he was struck and struck again with a sweeping, sharp object. Every stabbing just felt like a light touch as the pain slowly went away altogether. As more metal ripped through his skin, chipping his bones, and penetrated his soft pink intestines, all feeling for the world and his body left him. He didn't even feel his own life slip away as he drifted off.

Coyote inserted the knife into the mouth of the dead man. He slid it past his lips and through his tender teeth and lodged the dagger here and there. The sharp silver edge cut out bright rose petals around the tongue and gums. It all bled and came apart like a mangled fruit, pooling with blood until it overflowed out of his lips.

A dark rainbow of black, red, and brown ran all over the floor and Coyote's sweat-shined face. It was the first time the young man had smiled in a while. He couldn't remember last time he'd felt so proud of himself.

He sighed in relief. He didn't want to kill. But killing was just a social construct. Killing was just a different word for the same transformation. His crooked smile dripped with rivers of red. His eyes glowed like a hungry hawk.

"Maximus! You may come now." His voice echoed again. Short of breath, he yelled. But it wasn't until he lowered his voice, letting his larynx loose like a wild animal screech, that he finally heard the jogging strides of his servant. The footsteps came quickly. The feet scampered and made loud echoes in the quiet halls.

Coyote stared at the mess at his feet, wishing to wash his hands clean of the blood and scrub his memory that the mess ever happened. He wanted to run away into the hills to live with the wolves and beasts forever—maybe they'd understand him better. Those beasts and scavengers and coyotes who lurked in the night—maybe they would accept him as one of their own.

He stood still, paralyzed by the stench and sight of the piled remains on the floor. He tilted his head in wonder at the rich mix of deep colors. Velvet burgundy, shades of red, deep red, and bright tones of brown—all hues he'd never seen come together before quite like this. He was amazed. It was the most beautiful work of art he'd ever seen, and it seemed to move and spread across the floor, unfolding before his very eyes as if it lived! The puddle of blood wished to spread its wings and fly, growing and painting all on its own! The crumpled flesh wanted to change color and put on a show for the emperor. Coyote stared. He couldn't turn his head away from the most beautiful art he'd ever seen. And it was all made by his own hand. He could no longer hear the servant's steps approaching him. The whole world was a blank void that surrounded his great work of art.

It was an expansive wonder of secrets. So lively and loud. Coyote's lips twisted into a glowing moon. The emperor stood above his creation, looked down on it, and smiled. He smiled even though it hurt. He smiled because it hurt. What else would you do?

***

Maximus continued to yell the emperor's name from the bottom of the staircase. The man in the ratty robe stayed still. Coyote's vision granted thoughts that ripped portals to unfound worlds. Black holes to lights of new color, deeper black, completely dodging death.

"Coyote! Coyote! Master, what is this issue? Please...." But the cries were lost to the dry air; his ears were shut to the servant's calls, lost in endless thought.

I can see this mess—this same stinking pile of waste walked in here on its own on two legs, with its own two eyes, and with its own little will to power. Well, where is that 'will to power' now? How has that willpower served you, Your Holiness? Hm. It has all been broken and rebuilt, reshaped better by me. I can see it, yet it cannot see me. What is God but power and love? And I am both of those things—the new creator. What once had a will to live no longer lives. This pile of rose-blood has no more secrets to tell. It only moves when I kick it. It had never been a thing this whole time, for it's new. But it's nothing. Maybe nothing, but I guess food for the birds and the beasts—but nothing more! And he dies, yet I live right now. This beautiful mess of color and flesh used to be a person. But there is no desire that exists in this pool of blood on my marble floor. And yet, here I stand. I know what I want to do, and I can do it. I can do what I want. I now can always do what I please.

Coyote smiled to himself. *Yes, I called him 'The Creator,' knowing I'd be the one to create my own picture of him. I architected the end of his lineage, ending his family's rich history with a few swipes of a dirty knife. His ancestors, his lost father, his mourning mother, and all his siblings—they all looked down on me until they had to look up. But villains always despise heroes. Villains project their own wicked reflections onto the good people that oppose them. I created a ceiling that capped how far his ancestors could fly. His whole bloodline is forever finished. And I did that. They're all gone, lost in the natural cycle of things. They're all hopeless. I created that. What a wonderful life I live. What an exciting story to tell!*

The young man jumped and yelped like a spooked animal as he felt something grip his shoulder. He gripped the knife and shook his blade back and forth and swiveled his head. But all he could see was his servant standing there scared, backing away with mortal terror in his eyes.

"Master, are you alright? What happened? Are you—"

"I made 'The Creator' in my own image. I'm fine. I'm well. I'm *better* than fine. I'm actually great!" He approached the man with the bloody knife still showing, widened eyes, and a crescent smile. His face told a story of manic ambition that could never tire.

"Oh, don't back away, Maximus. You're not one of them. You *aren't* them. Don't be afraid." The servant obeyed. "I stand here now with my own will, energy, and the *fervor* of *life* in my hands to do what I wish! I feel a spark. I feel born again!" He spoke rapidly, barely breathing between words. "Maximus, I was *attacked*. He brutally assaulted me. He came up here, and I... I sent *you* away in full trust that I'd be safe with him! How foolish I was to ignore you, my only faithful friend! I am so sorry! So... so... sorry...." Coyote's voice became bleak and slow and sad. From a certain angle, it looked like his eyes glistened with tears. "Why would they want to hurt me? I still can't understand why people want to see me bleed. After all I've been through... I send *my only* trusted advisor, my only *friend*, to leave me alone with a hungry wolf. There are too many of them, Maximus. Too many wolves with greedy eyes." Coyote slammed his fist. "Too many! And after all I've been through—all of this, this thing called life that has only been cruel to me—I'm still the hunted one. I remain on the warpath, and yet I want to go home! I'm tired, Maximus. I'm tired, and they only want to take more. I have nothing left to give, and yet they want more." He whispered with tears in his eyes. "I never asked to live in the jungle. And yet, I was born into it."

Coyote roared and yelped. But his cries only bounced off the white ceiling just above him. The servant stood and shivered, waiting for him to stop crying and yelling like a mad animal.

Coyote's animal urge was to gut his scared servant right there and carve him up into tiny pieces. He could smell the fear rising from his skin. The knife he gripped was hot and thirsty for more. He jolted, then he stopped himself. Something held him back from more violence, and to the servant, it looked more like a psychotic spasm—he had no idea his life was in danger. Coyote's eyes spoke of nothing, seemed to say nothing, devoid of anything meaningful, looking at some distance far away.

Human eyes could never catch the pictures in Coyote's mind. Both men stood in silence as blood spread across the floor. And it spread. Coyote's head slowly bobbed up and down—lifeless eyes.

"How's your family, Max?"

"They're well, sir. They're, they're all well."

"And the little one? How old is she now?"

"She's four. Four-years-old last month."

"That's great. That's really awesome. What about your wife?"

"She's great. Oh, she told me to say 'hi,' by the way."

"That's nice of her. She's always nice! Please give her my regards."

"I will, Sir. I'll let her know. As for the—"

"The what?"

"The attack, Sir. You were attacked. Are you okay? Should I fetch for someone?"

"Oh, that's just one of many. They've always come—those hungry beasts that only want *things*. They don't want to actually *be* important. They just want to feel it. Power's always been fluid, and right now, I hold a large tub of that liquid gold that everyone seems to want. It's not me that they want—it's my skin. But they wouldn't want this pain, even if they got me. And yet, today, I remain standing over my—" Coyote looked down at the still-swarming pool of blood at his feet. He gently kicked the heap of robes crumpled at his feet. "I stand over my assailant today. Triumphant. Tomorrow, I may be where they lay—all those envious mosquitoes itching to suck whatever honest blood I have left." Coyote continued to cry. "I could turn out like him."

"Sir, you shouldn't talk like that. It gives way to dangerous thoughts. It gives the universe ideas."

"Please call me by my name, Max. I do have a name, you know."

"Coyote, those words are poison. You shouldn't speak of such dangers. Otherwise, they may come true."

"But it's all true. All of it is. The lies. The lonely and forgotten souls. The cold streets where no one cares. All children get left behind. It's all wrong! I've seen the evils of this world. Many others have, too, but no one knows them like I do. I dance with them every night. I've gazed into the chasm deeply for so long, and it glared back at me. There is nothing more sinister than that—being a giver in a world that only wants to take everything. Therein lies the secret; we want what we can't have, or can't have for long, while the power we were all born with we ignore and throw by the wayside like garbage. But I don't mind the constant windfall that humanity is. I don't have any more mind to give. I don't mind the coming seasons of people and places. I don't know what I mind any more, really, because everything burns…. And, besides, I have no mind left to pay." Coyote cleared his throat and looked down at his dripping knife. Splotches of his skin were still stained with the blood of another man. "I'm glad your family's well. It brings me joy to know they're happy. I know you're a good man and a great father, and your loved ones are blessed to have you in their lives, as you are so grateful for them. I hope to keep it that way. Stay grateful for what you have. If you can clean up this mess, I'll give you a bucket of thumb-sized gold nuggets to take home to your family. I'm sure your wife might like some gifts, and your children would love to see their father tonight. I want you to get home as soon as you can and only report back to me when you're comfortable and rested tomorrow. Understand? I want you and your family to be comfortable, happy, and rested!"

"It will be done, Master."

"Call me Coyote! That's my name!"

"Yes, Coyote. I can do that."

"So the mess cleaned up? Your kids with all the sweets and toys they'd ever want? Your wife with a nice new bracelet? Show her you love her; don't just tell her.

Hire people to fix your roof, too—I know it's been leaking. Can you do all of that? For me?"

"For you. Of course. Yes, I can absolutely do that for you."

"Good. And by the way, I am going to skip my writing tonight and go on a walk late into the evening, maybe even until dawn. When you leave, please let the guards know that I'll be gone for a while on my walk."

"I will let them know, Coyote. Thank you. Thanks for everything."

"Good. And—oh! Have them bring my reserve soldiers here to keep close watch around the house. I want another guard inside for when I return to sleep the next day. I may be out for a while. Put three or so—no, five—around the property to keep watch. Another one inside the house, please, ensuring my safe return."

"It will all be done. I will make sure of it."

"Oh, and my safe sleep!"

"Of course, Sir."

"Oh, and Maximus?"

"Yes, Sir—Coyote?"

"Enjoy your gold. Enjoy your family. Embrace them and enjoy every second with them. That time you have with those little loved ones is precious. Spend it wisely."

"I know." The servant nodded, holding back tears. "Thank you. Thank you for everything."

The emperor shuffled back into his room, the one with the mural of the great man and the small boyish bed and the giggling flame. He blew it out and let the smoke-soaked air of the dark fill his nostrils. He closed his eyes and thought about his plan. He even smiled in his sleep as he drifted deeper downward, sinking into a blank abyss.

He rested for a while with his crimson dagger in his sheets. He always felt most comfortable closest to the edge.

Chapter 17
Mikalla Leaves Forever

"I don't want you to say it again."

"So, what could you possibly want to say, Jani?"

"Don't tell me you love me."

"But I do love you."

"Stop saying that. Just stop."

"But I do love you," Mikalla said. And he meant it. He meant every word and always told the truth, even when he lied. He wanted all of the woman's love and the fruit of the wondrous life to come with it. Everything in life and all the smiles and sunrises he wanted and saw with pupils the size of stars. But The Last Conjurer was still just a man.

"I know you love me, but your love has never been enough for me. Maybe that's why you've loved me so; you're ambitious without a cause. *So ambitious,* in fact, you wanted to do something that even *your* stubbornness never thought possible beyond some stupid dream—love an unlovable person. You are even more ambitious than I am, Mikalla, and I want it *all.* You want more than me, and I'm, well, I'm a greedy pig. You can't be satisfied with some fangirl. You're a human, maybe more so than me. It's too *much. You're* too much."

"But I know you want love, Jani. You always have. I know it because I've grown to know you, your struggles and trauma, and when I see and hear you, it's pure pleasure. Your voice is the grace that never relents. It is the gi—"

"It's madness, Mikalla. That's what it is! It's madness, and it's *crazy. You're* crazy. I need more. I've always needed more than just some kisses and kind words. So then, why all this? You make me look sane! I mean, how is that possible? You're an addict, and I'm your addiction. How could that be?"

"It's why the moon follows the sun, Jani. It's why the night grows deep purple, and maybe why we all need the light, especially in the dark." Mikalla looked down at his feet, at the glistening floors of the marble-white purgatory all around him. He hoped it was all a bad dream. But whatever it was, he needed to get out. He knew he had no more stories to tell, but he had one more to live out—one more death to die. He had to escape somehow.

Jani made a stinking face. Her body shivered. But her thoughts were so limited to the walls around her, caged in a tiny room with vaulted ceilings and running water. Because she could never escape her fate, all she ever wanted to do was escape. Maybe it gave her joy just to pound at the walls of her existence and gnash her teeth at the bars in the prison of her mind, yelling and screeching for a window or some ray of light.

Her body always knew that Mikalla would never be enough. That's why she kept him around; he'd never satisfy her. But no one man ever could. Mikalla's quivering chest knew this about Jani, but his lips never spoke of it. His stories could only hint at the shadow. He could never know that *one* thing—that his only love, his greatest joy, that pure person so profound, would never love him back. It all was a purposeful mistake. He was just another joke the gods laughed at.

So Mikalla hoped to free others from their chains, despite not having the key to his own shackles. He did this for some impulse or reason beyond his control, and it decided how and why he lived and how and why he died.

Jani wished for something to be different, as she always had. Being a great mind herself, she knew how to poke and prod at great minds to use them like playthings. "What is freedom?" She asked. "It must be a great story, or peace, or painting, or *some* happily ever after, or *love*—pure and profound love, or the pleasure of drinking wine and laughter, right? Right? Freedom must be some sort of love. Freedom has to be one of those wonderful pleasures by the sun, right, Mikalla? Something has to mean freedom for me... and for *us*. Otherwise, what's the point inside our little lives, doing little things we're forced to do with all our little great powers as people? So what is it? What is freedom? What *is it*? It must be something! Freedom!"

Mikalla looked down. His tired eyes told of a thousand ventures, a million pains, and a sorrow that saw no end. "There is no freedom. Freedom is a lie told by a liar and the many liars before him. That lie of freedom gets passed on from generation to generation, parent to child, but it's the only thing we can cling to; it is at times the hope of it all we have, and yet we've never really had it."

And Jani teared up at the thought of the great prison that was her life. Her eyes welled, and her voice cracked. She tried to spit out a word, but it sounded like a grunt. "Th—there must be stories! Stories, Miki. Miki, you must have somethingbecause if Idon't get an answer, Idon'tIdon'tknowwhatI'do." Jani sobbed. She finally broke; her body tired of putting up a fake front. Her chest heaved, and her red eyes strained as thick layers of tears streamed down her cheeks.

Two broken people hunched and cried together. Maybe that was love.

"I would tell you to keep living, Jani, and live as best you can. But we no longer live. All I ever tried to do was be a light. I had a flame in me, and I don't even know what fire is. But with that flame, I illuminated the murals on the walls in the dark labyrinth of life."

"What does that even *mean*? Mikalla! So you don't have an answer?"

"That is my answer. It always has been."

"Then where do I go? This pain is not enough for me. The prison of my mind is no—this prison needs to go and I need to leave. Yes, I needtoleave. I need to leave righnow." She sobbed. "I needoleevrighnaugh."

"No matter how far you run in this world, you'll always just run into a larger prison caging you in."

Jani hid her teary eyes in her hands. "Then what do I do? What is this? Where are we? Tell me!" Her voice swelled to a high-pitched whimper like a dying bird screeching to be saved. "Tellmetellmetelll… me. Tell me!" She sniffled. "I need an honest answer…."

"I don't know," Mikalla said. "That's my honest answer. I can't tell you how to escape. *But* I can tell you that we created a future—*some* future—where all our actions meant something. If not to last forever, then to at least walk the earth and be his own person. We're only creatures, Jani, and together, we created a new one of our own, *a life* that can walk and talk and move around the world while he learns what awaits him. Maybe someday he'll find someone he loves as much as I've loved you."

"And, and I get it…. And you're only a creature that loves me. Yes, yeah…. I know, Mikalla. I get it. I truly get it. But you know that's not enough—not for me. I want more. I've always wanted *more*. I can't help it!"

Mikalla's tired eyes only gleaned the surface of what he could really see. Those tired and troubled eyes just passed over the true forms of every object they came across. They scanned and searched for nothing. They moved slowly all around and could not make out anything; they couldn't see past a simple shape or shadow. Finally, his lips told what his eyes saw and spoke of for so long, what his body longed to say, and what his mouth refused to publish.

"I know you want more, Jani. I do, too. We all do, and we always will. Not just you and me, but the rest of us. That's our prison—wanting more. And if prison's so bad, then so is life itself. But I like lighting my flame and letting it grow to burn. This prison doesn't have to be so bad if you can continue to destroy and create. But I don't know. That's for you to decide." He sobbed.

They both cried and shed more tears, sniffling before Mikalla got up and left, up from the couch and away from the knife, his wife, his life, and the past. His iron shackles melted away as he strode toward the light, away from all his mistakes and missteps, toward the door where the sun shone through tall windows, glaring white and glinting yellow rays. Mikalla reached for the handle of the door. Maybe he'd disappear. Maybe it was peace on the other side of that door. Maybe he'd feel peace for once, for the first time since he was a young boy, maybe ever. But it wasn't peace he sought. He was never scared to live, never scared to die. Comfort and safety were not constructs of his mind, only dreams of great stories that spoke of high heights and glorious gods. No, peace never spoke to him, nor did he search for it ever. Peace was a lie, and he knew it. He put his hand to the cold knob of the door and twisted. Only Jani's sobs could be heard as the door slid open to silence.

The man, the boy, the young and dead soul only ever sought to search and find more.

He left all that came before him, all he did before then, and all he would do afterwards; because he wasn't scared to love and live, he held no fear of dying.

He walked out the door and into a light unknown, and he liked not to know. *Why*, he thought, *stay in the same known place when there is a whole world beyond for all time*? The ultimate light, not the dark, took Mikalla's body. Where he went he wouldn't know, and he liked that;

he preferred that. And he went on, past his past life, passing on to a place he wanted to go—elsewhere.

Maybe it mattered. Maybe it meant nothing. No matter what it meant, he went on and left.

Chapter 18

A Brat Gets Lit

Metzli struggled to open her eyes that morning. Her stomach churned full of sores. She felt bloated and slow, sweating—everything hurt to touch or move. The sun glinting the windows spoke of a new day, but her body wanted to hide and cling to the covers. Even in the bright light of morning, a dark cloud hung in her soul, warning of a storm she couldn't avoid. She felt heavy and cold with all her jewelry and gems she kept on her body. They bound her wrists, strangled her fingers, and choked her neck like golden shackles.

She wanted to break out of her chains and fly away from her cage, but she was just so tired. She waited in bed for the sacred single man who saw the good in her. He was a powerful man—the High Priest of Idaza—and she loved the way he complimented her; even his simple smile excited her. He made her feel special with his words laced in silver. She loved it all and wanted to do anything he said, so long as he would give her what he promised— ultimate power. She wanted and pleaded and *needed* him to command her, make her body work, and make her hands do things.

But the morning sun brimmed a bit brighter, and Metzli's body jolted. She couldn't hold still and allow a man, no matter how mighty he may be, to take her sense of pride as an esteemed person of nobility. She was rich. But was she really rich if everyone around her had all the same things as her? All the empty skulls and sinful souls that skulked the wings of the shell of the royal palace droned on as rich idiots, *each one stupider than the last,* she thought. They all believed in nothing but fine things and endless wine, shiny parties made for mornings of wretched headaches shunning the harsh light of the forgiving sun. They all urged this cycle, this *endless* cycle, of drinking and debauchery and entangled bodies, surfing skin, smiling and moaning until dark met dawn, in which they'd all meet again in a silk web the following night to no end. They took drugs to help with the nausea and stomach aches, hoping one more time to put on a better costume dress than the night before, for either more fun or more pleasure or more fun. More fun. More pleasure. All the wealthy nobles really owned nothing but their own empty pride.

She would attend those parties for a short while before she got bored and retreated back to her private room in the palace.

And she could not take the silence of the black curtains covering bright windows any longer. She huffed and called out to a random servant of the palace scurrying about. "Hey…."

They met and exchanged pleasantries. She didn't recognize this person with their hood on. But the servant knew who she was.

"Where is Lupus?"

"Lupus? Who is Lupus? You ask of his whereab—"

"Yes! Yes," Metzli cut the lowly servant off. "Can someone—can *you* get someone that knows where he is and please deliver him to me? I've been asking forever now, and I can't contact my associate. Hurry and go get him! He's the High Priest of Idaza. Fetch him. Now and go!"

The humble servant just nodded in silence, waiting for the angry woman to stop speaking. He nodded slowly and hid his face. "Madam, I have fetched for him, his assistants, his ushers, and all the rest of His Grace's compatriots on numerous occasions…. There's—there's practically a whole search party looking for him. They're all trying desperately to bring him to you. But I do have a report."

"*And*?" Metzli kept her arms crossed by strained by her black sleeves. "So what's your report?"

"Did you say he was an associate of yours?"

"What the hell does that matter to *you, young boy*? That doesn't concern you. I asked you *a question*. Now, answer me, or you will be reported to the emperor himself."

"Oh, my sincerest apologies. I didn't realize—"

"So what's your report on Lupus?"

"It is reported, Madam, that he has been engaged in a prayer ceremony. It seems, as my sources tell me, he has gone alone into deep meditation. He may be in a deep slumber, away on his pilgrimage to commune with the gods. Holy works, Madam. He is clearly engaged in holy works, indeed."

Metzli kept her arms crossed, her face tight and twisted. She stood stout as a statue and pondered her next move. *This servant speaks clearly—possibly too clearly for someone with no education from the lower classes.... Why does he speak so softly yet so strongly? His whole life is meant only to serve me, the iron woman who carved her own path. I'm as strong as steel and have the power to have him executed for a simple mistake; so why does he speak to me like I am his equal? What will I do if I can't reach the high priest? What next? Why did I hinge so much trust in one man? Ugh! Stupid. Maybe, then, I will continue to cozy up to Coyote's servant; his name was... Maxim... Maxelus... Maximus! Yes, Maximus. I could tell he liked me, and I can seduce him and get information that way. Yes, that way, I can get what I want. That That servant is the weakest link. But what did Lupus have planned for me, anyway?* She tightened her torso, arms, and jaw, grinding her teeth with a twisted face, while the servant stood unmoved. Her twisted forehead showed a deep disquiet with the servant's answer—this stupid, lonely, and subservient man had no business being her messenger. She felt that she'd seen and spoken with this type of person before—the kind that only reveals more questions the longer you pry and the more you dig for what you want. "Reveal your face, slave."

"I thank you for your grace, but I am no slave, Madam."

Metzli's face reverted to a confused look. "But you are a servant, no?"

"I am a servant, in that I serve people, Madam. But I am no slave—not a slave to you, and not a slave to anyone. If you choose to call me that abhorrent word, *Madam*, then know that I am only in bondage to my own life that the gods gave me as one of their cruel jokes. But not even to the gods am I a slave. I was once in bondage, and now I am master of myself." Metzli was taken aback at the young man's words. She knew no servant who could speak like that. Her chest fluttered, and her stomach tumbled at his powerful speech.

Maybe she loved him like a son already; maybe all her life she was meant to hear those splendid words spoken that way. But she still couldn't see his face, and maybe she did know him. She thought she did. For a second, her soul snapped at a memory of a boy long ago; he had a soft face with fierce eyes, sharp jaws, and cheeks she never got to touch.

The servant continued to talk to himself as if no one could hear him. "If I could ever be called a slave, I am locked in eternal bondage to the crooked imaginations who conjured up the gods before me. No one has any say over what I am. I am inevitable, and I just don't know what that inevitability is or what it will be. That's the trick that keeps on tricking; it's the only thing I can't get away from, and I don't know what that is." His voice trailed off, and he looked into the distance as if they were atop a mountain.

The woman—gilded in a veil of glitzy jewels around her torso, neck, limbs, hands, ears, and shoes—fixed on the faceless man. She must've known him, had to have known him, but couldn't quite locate the face or the name. Something from her memory knew the young man—she recognized that *tone*, that pattern of speech, that truthful voice that sounded scared and proud. But she couldn't see his face. She was a prisoner shackled in gold, unlike the servant—dressed simply. But she wasn't so foolish to think that this was any servant. In fact, she knew. She knew this was not a servant, but some other type of figure who was not there to serve anyone but himself. She was too smart not to see through the disguise. She fidgeted and grinded her teeth as silence sat between them for a while. *Why is he not saying anything? What should I say*? Her frustrated body shook more, waiting to reach a breaking point when her blood would boil over. But she had enough of all the fidgeting and angst that bubbled just under the surface of her still-soft skin. This... *servant*—this lowly servant seemed to rekindle a magic made long ago. *But that is no servant.* "Reveal yourself, Sir. Remove your hood and face me."

"I told you, and I made myself very clear."

"Please," Metzli bowed, "remove your hood and show your full face to me."

A thousand questions came to the man's mind, and he chose to wisely keep quiet. He chose to stay still. He knew that, for once, he had the power. She wanted something from him. She asked; she wanted something from him, and in doing so, she gave him the power to accept or refuse what she wanted on his terms. The woman that dominated his dreams and snuck into his nightmares bowed down to him.

"Sir, please…. Please don't make me call the guard—uhm, oh! I wouldn't call the guard. I wouldn't call the guard on you."

She smiled, and everything stopped. A mighty tingle trickled through the man's veins. It was some electric throbbing, something he hadn't felt in a long while. It wasn't a lonely or angry feeling, but rather a tinge of peace, of harmony and joy, some spiritual song that played when he gazed upon the woman's smile. And she smiled like a girl and not a lady. And he knew that girl, the one with the dreams of living in luxury and not having to ever work or want for a thing. He pictured her smile with closed eyes. It pierced the history of his life. It was a pleasant memory, but those memories opened wounds and sliced him, something like a sweet scalpel. There was so much joy in the cuts, so much sweetness in the slice.

But that smile was in the past. Her sunlit teeth showed a window only to what was. His memories and feelings stayed the same, but time moved on. He made up his mind.

They both had conflicting goals—only one could win in a tussle of two in the jungle. Both people were rotten. Both of them were selfish and cold. But only one of them had a knife.

The spirit may overcome the blade in the end, but the sharpened blade still cuts skin. Skin—soft and smooth skin like Metzli's—was attractive and proud. But soft-beating flesh only yielded to the blade's edge. It was Metzli that inspired the vigorous flame of Coyote's youth. She was who he thought about, who he pictured when he was lonely and locked away and times were so tough. And then she left and did this to herself.

The man took off his hood and showed all the slices on his face. Metzli gasped and backed away. Though her heart was cold, it thawed as she looked at the boy she knew who grew up too fast and got hurt too easily.

But nothing could hurt Coyote any longer. It was Metzli's turn.

"Coyote? Why? How? What happened?"

Every step she took back, he took three toward her. She pleaded at first. She scrambled and started to run once she felt his intentions were not pure; those were angry footsteps pacing right at her. She yelled and huffed. She begged for answers and breathed heavier with wide eyes, looking for a way out or a person to help. When she looked back, she saw his face one last time. She knew it was Coyote, but those boyish eyes she knew from long ago had frozen over. The color was gone, the joy and innocence left. He was stripped of all, and left in the shell was a maniac who had no aim but to hurt.

Metzli felt a shooting pain in her side. It took the wind out of her lungs. She tried to yell, but her throat could barely make a sound. Her whole face bent and melted into agony, her mouth wide, eyes rolled back, brows raised, gasping for air. But there was no escape. She cried out in a soft pitch, trying to run and yell, yet her legs stopped working and her voice went mute. All her gold could not buy her new life, all her money couldn't buy her more time, and none of her beauty or jewelry could bring back all the memories that would fade as quickly as her blood left her body.

Plunk. Shink. A groan. Soft skin is broken again. This time her heart was pierced with the edge. *Shik. Ssik. Ssssssik.*

The light dimmed quicker with every time the knife jutted into her tender side, her bony back. Her hopes for new horizons poured out of her mouth. The shooting pain felt better the more blood she lost. She watched from afar her entire existence pop like a bubble. The dagger harvested no gold; no crystal shards fell out of her gut; no green emeralds were dug up out of her intestines—just purple ink and pink dermis and bits of blood, feeding rivers that led to lakes and oceans that spread across the white marble floor.

The struggling soon stopped, and all went silent. Only hollow echoes could be heard, and no one was near enough to listen.

Her eyes were open, but she could not see. She lay on her back as she felt less and less. Her limp body lay in blood. The red puddles and creeks were outshined by her sparkling ruby rings. Her smooth skin was no longer recognizable. She covered herself in shiny things and colored rocks that could not protect her; those rocks and golden strings and useless pretty things would live far beyond her dying flesh. She was stabbed another time. Again, the blow of the dagger struck her. Another swipe of the knife cracked her ribs. Coyote's eyes looked like greedy voids, never satisfied, always motivated, chasing a goal he could never get.

A gem wanted to be worshiped; a mere person can't be worshiped. But a fine garment of silk or satin can be displayed for all time. A porous body of wrinkles that quivered and fidgeted was only as valuable as how tightly it was bound. She woke up a woman with ideas and fears, and she died an hour later as a bulbous sack of slaughtered meat, rotting. What was a human's blood but a vehicle to get more garments, see more sights, explore more pleasures, drink more wine, and feast on fatter duck?

Metzli was stabbed and stabbed again. She was stabbed and sliced once more, again a slice, another chunk of skin went to skunk, no shriek but a plunk of a dying sound, a swan's song Metzli sang as her dim green eyes faded to a forest hue, and then all got quiet but for the plunk of the knife.

Sssik.

Ssssssik.

Ssssssik.

Silence.

One last heavy breath.

Ssssssik.

Rivers of red. Eyes rolled back dead. Nothing said. Words meant nothing to the dead. They couldn't hear, couldn't say what they wanted, and couldn't choose their bed when they finally lay to rest. Metzli—the woman—was no longer. She was dead. The servant who stabbed her to death was alive, and his name was Coyote. The servant. The prisoner. The emperor. The same person who escaped back into bondage to kill and create after all those he held dear were killed by fate. So he was just a part of that same wheel that killed his parents, their parents, and it would kill him too. He would go back to dust too. He liked to act and spin the wheel a little faster.

He was the fate of the winds. He was the fate of the flame.

Metzli lay dead as Coyote stood and watched the life seep from her veins, drain from her pale emerald eyes, spill onto the palace floor, stained forever. It was funny how none of her jewels and silver could change the color of her blood.

Coyote looked at the messy pile he made. Now he had his pyre. As soon as it dried a bit, he would have his final fire pit.

***

He went to work whittling with his kindling tools quickly. The whole might of this man bent on one goal: fire. The blitz of the ravenous flame set free on a scarce earth until one day it may be consumed, maybe—maybe there could be a life anew. But for now, Coyote just worked and worked in the dry air of the palace halls until he saw a spark fly. It was bright and brief like a shooting star. Gone. He thought he saw something. Another spark flew. It caught the cloth on the ground. Coyote dropped his jaw. He marveled at the moment and smiled at the memory of the spark. What potential that one spark had! It could've changed history…. But Coyote would make sure that its life was not wasted.

He bit his lip and whittled harder, creating more sparks. His eyes glowed. All the visions that led in his head started with small sparks. Tiny tinders were still flames. More sparks were born. They flew and speckled the black cloth on the ground.

Pop.

Pop.

Crackle.

Coyote saw all these hungry fires full of life and didn't want to see their lives end so quickly. No! He wanted those little sparks to come into being and grow. Fire can only be greedy. A flame is either ambitious or dead. That is the only way to live.

Fire is the greatest teacher.

We admire what can kill us. That's why we love the flame and stare at its smoke.

His yellow eyes glowed in the shadow of a large statue. He stared at the tiny sparks. They chewed holes through the clothes until they came together and started to chortle. It was a small civilization of sparks that met all at the same time—Coyote was the god but could not control everything. The smell was deep and dense, but familiar. Once the clothes lit, the dry flesh caught fire. The smoke was black. The flame grew.

Coyote smiled.

The stench was brighter, denser, and deeper in the back of his nostrils. He didn't cough, but his body seized up in many weird ways. This crumpled pile of flesh and cloth was only a pyre. It was just a birthplace for new life, and the young man created it. The society grew too populous for its pastures. The Emperor of Idaza disapproved of this royal palace where all the wealthy vagrants would haunt. It would now submit to the whims of the flame. It would burn. It would grow, but only through death.

Coyote's mind went as wild as the rapid flame danced and devoured the corpse; the blood smoked, and the incense was intoxicating. The fire grew. The fire jumped and laughed. It blazed, red wings on the flying red falcons everywhere. The flame raged on. Coyote smiled wider. His eyes were consumed by the flame that glowed orange and red as blood.

Oh! What a story this is, Father! What a tale told. A true story. It's a story for you, Dad. I know you would appreciate the beauty of this drama—and it is a drama for the ages, one that could live in the minds of people for as long as they breathe... and then countless generations to come. But now, instead of telling the story, Dad, I get to live it! I am the story; I am a part of the glorious history of the burning you so spoke of long ago! To countless souls that drank in every word as a nurturing nectar for their souls.... I am that one. I am the actor in this play, the god who created the first food. I granted man the flame! I act in this story you laid out in your real, real life. You died, and you didn't have to....

Coyote shed a tear. He thought about his dad. He saw flashes of his face and his smile. He was a pure man. He was a man rich in spirit. And Coyote cried more at the memory of his father. His heart was twisted by the tears. He didn't want to sob, but maybe the tears were some solution to the fire. He was tired of crying. So, Oh! He grew angry at life again. He grew angry at the day he was born and the people that brought him unto this wretched world ruled by physics.

But I live, and you lay rotting in the earth. Your stories were as nutritious to the people as your corpse is to the nearby oak trees. You may feed a few plants now, but I act on the living, the breathing beings of the present, and all of them feel my presence. Coyote was blinded by the glaring light of the growing flame. As the flame grew, the hallway of the palace shrouded in gray and black. The smoke was thick and toxic. The flame grew to the size of a small sun and heated the whole area. Heat. Dry, black heat spread quickly, suffocating everyone that didn't run.

I just don't feel like anything else matters right now but my actions and my rebellion. I detest all radical teachings, all power against me, and all the power that even I wield. I despise power among the hands of man, and so I wield it only to disperse it, extinguish it, and let the hand of nature carry all life! In that way, I am nature. Yes, Dad, I am nature. Maybe it matters. Oh, maybe it matters, Dad. Ayyhg. Maybe it has a bearing on the future of others. The whole kingdom.... I know nothing of great fates. Therefore, I am a torn and broken man, just as you were at the end of your life. Yes, I know how you died. You were a puppet of the state. I am The Puppeteer. I am the Lord. You paved the way for me, and so I have become greater than you! I have surpassed you with my own skill. I have written for this kingdom to be free. They have been in bondage... but even broken people can create new life! This is what I write for.

I stand for nothing—not even myself. I watch this flame burn as my only light. It warms me in the crisp air of the lonely morning. I command the most sophisticated people in the known world—millions of them—as I stand on the shoulders of giants long past. And yet, I can't help but think you were the greatest giant, Dad. Even as a flawed man, I don't think you've made any mistakes, and in your many flawed stories, you've spun gold. The masses love flaws. They love flawed and evil characters because it reflects their broken spirits, just like mine, Dad. That messenger—The true Last Conjurer, My Father, Mikalla, The One—could not make a mistake without making it perfect.

But now I light a fire on the dead body of a girl I once loved. She burns, and soon, the immortal palace of culture, paintings, and other priceless art shall burn. But all of these pieces of culture will no longer be priceless as they burn to the ground.

With the palace up in smoke, becoming nothing but a great blaze, the commoners may see a great dance from afar. But no matter how distant this fire burns, it is near their hearts. Their souls will rejoice with a flame brighter than the sun, burning the past but never forgetting it. Stories…. Yes! Stories will live while the fire kills all else.

Father. Mikalla. Dad. Sacred storyteller, last of the great Conjurers, hear me this: all of your stories are just your own vain biographies. It seems as though I continue this great legacy of pennants with my own flame. Vanity. Yes, Dad, I am vain. I think I'm great. I know I am the best; that's what we share: a pride in our work.

I love you. I love these people. I love all humans who suffer, and all of them do.

I see this flame growing and latching onto the walls of the royal palace now…. I know this palace has been built over many generations. I respect it, but… oh! It's getting hot. It's hot like Hell. I need to run now.

***

Coyote looked at the burning body and lamented nothing, thought nothing, but smelled a thick stench. He smelled it all—death, life, and rebirth. He coughed and coughed and coughed as the flames rose higher. Finality. Finally, new life from death. All those wealthy nobles would have nowhere to sleep as their royal hotel burnt to the ground. But he still smiled as he stared into the void.

He chanted to himself while watching the flame burn.

Burning. Rotting. Blackening before his eyes. He could only speak a few words before the black smoke consumed the halls and the rest of the quarters, growing to an unquenchable figure that could never be satisfied. He liked it that way; he liked sweating under his robe; he liked the chaos, for what was beauty without chaos? His mind spun, and he couldn't think. It was a twister in his eyes, red and orange. He didn't think, and so he smiled. He liked doing things and not giving one thought to his actions. It felt better to act and not think.

A giant fire with a life of its own took rise. Maybe that's what his father would've wanted. He might not have cared—it was impossible to know. But flames, like the young emperor, were rebellious and selfish and unpredictable and explosive and greedy and ambitious. They were anxious and indiscriminately harsh, angry at the world, seeking only to consume it and kill everyone before dying. It had to serve itself to grow. It destroyed and burnt so much.

Coyote didn't care.

The young man broke a sweat by the furious flame. He only looked at it and inched backward with every hot gulp of the smoke. He created a being that could burn a human that had a colder heart. The growing flame had no manners, only goals, and its goals were unknown; its desire was always a mystery. It was all a beautiful musical never told.

Maybe it mattered. He whispered while he stared into the flame. He had a dancing twinkle in the gape of his pupils. He stood still and spoke to the burning body. He hoped it felt his pain but wished he hadn't killed it before it burned. He wished she felt the pain of the flame before she died. He watched Metzli's skin melt, her eyeballs pop and shrivel, and the whole room fill with smoke.

"You've never known the cold like I did."

He turned his head away from the smoke, coughing. He started to run as the blaze grew brighter. Even if he created the tiny tinder with his own hands, his new creation did not care about the emperor, the woman, the dead kings that haunted the palace, or the rest of the world. It would eat him alive if it could. It would eat him dead and melting. Fire was selfish that way: it just wanted to eat and breathe—human, all too human! These flames! We worship fire as the greatest tool, and yet it dances madly with no control, impartial, unjust, and uncaring to what it devours, only wanting more. It wants more; its desire burns hotter than its wiggling red body, expanding always before dying.

Everything burns. Even the burns die, though.

Coyote smiled. He laughed as he ran, not worrying about the crumbling ceiling and distant shrieking voices. The palace walls blackened and smoked before falling all around him.

Coyote ran and ran, feeling the heat stroke his back still after many paces past the hall. He might have been on fire himself. His back burned. It crept toward him as he rushed, dripping sweat in the dark stench. His small feet and strides rambled as the flame moved at its own pace, growing with fury and taking its time. It went white-hot. It went blue as white turned to black. It turned to demon-red after it burned the black. The quivering red storm ate marble busts of history's figures, figures once known and respected, now gone to the flame. Their stories—those great heroes—could only be told by mouth or pen now.

The fire ripped up antiques and fine linens and entire rooms of the kingdom's finest things, its priceless paintings in its most historic estate, the center of all control for five generations; the untouchable royal palace made of marble melted and burst brightly like the death of an ancient star. Maybe it mattered. Maybe it was chemistry and physics that moved with the mind.

He was a lone orphan when this palace rested and lived with a steady pulse, overseeing all who walked by its walls. He was a single man as it withered to ash, leaving only hot stones alone on blackened grounds. Dead. The fire lived as the great palace died. Noble spices and wines and stained-glass windows. It stood tall for centuries with pride and power. Coyote always felt alone looking up at it, skulking in its vast wings, speaking to the people it held over the many years of his short life. He imagined all the meetings and romantic ventures of courage and cowardice, beautiful and ugly to the eye. But he was alone through it. He was alone in burning it down, running away from the smoke and the heat.

He saw feminine men and masculine women coughing, screaming, and running through the halls helplessly as the ceiling caved in and the smoke thickened. He stabbed all of them. He drove his bloody blade deep into their faces and gouged their guts before scampering along and escaping the palace; their bodies would make great food for the flame. Their eyes were wide with fear before they darkened to death, rolling back, gasping and groaning as they bled before being burnt. The Emperor's Guard, who were paid well, all stood around the palace with pikes in hand, ready to kill any trespasser that dared stand in the way of the burning palace.

Coyote smiled at the vision of a greater future from the ground up.

It was a horrific dance of death and dreams. All the noble people gilded in gold accepted their fate as the smoke drowned their lungs, and they doubled on all fours, coughing their lives away, trapped in the gold palace, dying young with all their riches and wine. They all, like mad ants scurrying for safety, began to beg for the blade rather than the blaze. Getting killed by a human was more pleasant than melting to death while suffocating with lungs full of ash. The rest of the nobles that survived the fire scampered towards safety. But through a long dark hallway, there was a figure that stood still, facing them, watching them, waiting for them. But the figure at the end of the tunnel was an artist who loved people and overflowed with empathy. He wouldn't let them melt— the end to their stories was a knife. Over and over he killed them. He kept stabbing and smiling, finally releasing their screams from the world into a deep silence so their bodies could feel no burning and so their minds could bear no more anxiety. In this way, Coyote was their savior, blocking the way to the light, stabbing them in the dark, one after one—so much blood and smoke.

Coyote ran and stabbed his way out, every few steps encountering some rich bureaucrats on their knees pleading for a peaceful end. "Please, please, Sir…. Don't do this. Please!" And they screamed as they were stabbed. Their eyes rolled back, and their bodies lost feeling before the flame ate them. They died. They all looked like burnt ants, lifeless and twitching.

He choked and coughed as he finally found the wider halls of the palace. He ran past ancient pillars that collapsed into dust right after he passed them. The palace held the culture of a million lives, many great men and women warriors, and the quarters of kings long past. As the kid made his way through the grand entrance one more time, he looked back and smiled at what he created: a black burning mist of fire set ablaze—sometimes it was just as creative to destroy. Paintings, great oak tables, marble statues, piles of gold coins and glasswork, etchings and priceless jewels and literature, whole libraries of scrolls and stories, wine bottles of rich heavenly burgundy, all gone forever.

Coyote was sure word of the great fire would spread to kingdoms far and near. He didn't quite know how to tell the story or how to sell the story to the leaders of other kingdoms. But as the age of the merchant had replaced the monarchs of old, a new rule he had not planned on would usher in an age of its own. Maybe it would be great. Maybe it would matter. Maybe he could stay alive and not be assassinated.

He ordered half his guards to kill any remaining survivors escaping from the palace's demise. He told the other half of the guard to escort him back to his house. He paid each of them more than a king's ransom. What was a king to a gold coin?

After all, it was only a building that burned that day—many pieces of his city's past. But love and lust and death and greed and beauty would live on. He could never kill those eternal things, nor did he want to. Humans were beautiful on their own; humanity was wondrous, but society sucked. He only wanted to set ablaze something about himself, something big and grand so intertwined with who he was so that he could rise anew with a laugh.

Selfish? Evil? Maniacal? Whimsical? He couldn't figure out why he did things, just as he couldn't find an answer as to why in life there's only room to lose things and nothing to gain. So he burned the palace down.

He didn't have the answers. He only knew he was a man that could act. He couldn't think, and so he acted. And then, flanked with armed guards all the way on his walk back to his house, he thought of the story he would write, the myths he could conjure up for all the people from the city commons watching the black smoke billow into pink sky from all sides, a memory for all time. He would surely tell the story. He would pen a tale for the ages about a new dawn that had come, about rebirth, about a society devoid of decadence and filled to the brim with fury and ambition. *Yes*!

Yes, that would be his narrative. An open horizon for all to look toward as they went about and created their own meanings for his tales, thinking about their own future, their children, and their legacy in a world so broken. A thinking population. A critical mass of people that only searched and strived, never complacent, always aggressive to learn the truth. *That* would be his story.

And when he arrived at his house, he thanked his guards and paid each of them handsomely, making them rich beyond anyone else in the kingdom. The emperor strode up to his room alone. His voice echoed in the wide halls of his childhood home. He took in a deep, clear breath and got his pen. He cleared his throat and wiggled his head. His leg twitched once. He wanted to create great words that moved multitudes of people forever and ever.

He took another breath and looked down at his work. His eyes went dark at the possibilities. Endless stories he could make, infinite human tales he could tell. But he decided to write finally and wrote one tale—that's all any one writer could do. His pen started to spill ink on the page after a time when the smoke was far away. He could see it out his window but chose to speak about the future instead of the past. Blood didn't matter to him unless it pumped life.

He handed out buckets of gold coins to each of his imperial guards. But betrayal, murder, and infidelity could never be stopped, no matter the money it cost.

Coyote wrote. He wrote in the dark and the light, by candle and wispy smoke, smelly wax, and conjured up a great story. By the lonely dim of dawning dusk through his black windows came words of all kinds, a wild, animalistic compulsion, an urgent need to have his insights and emotions fly from his heart.

He didn't want his people to suffer. He just wanted to give them a way to deal with their suffering. He hoped they would laugh at the pain but suffer all the same. There was no cure for the human condition, but there was a way to lift them to a higher plane of being.

He wrote. In the dark, he continued to write. When he took breaks, he nervously bit his pen and thought of his next words. He disappeared into the page. The pen laid spidery lines and black webs on the white page.

The pen struck the page again.

Another pen stroke, one less thought to think about. Coyote wrote more. His pen laid out a picture of sins and stories that would fulfill the hungry souls of the commoners for years to come. And the story about the ultimate burning of the kingdom's old political capital would give way to a new capital of culture. He created a story for people to tell their own. He bled black ink from his childhood, his adolescence, his young adulthood, his pleasure and pain that sang songs of life defying death, singing with laughter evil, the perfect mix of the world they knew and the world beyond.

He wrote.

Dimly by the flame, he wrote. It was all of his suffering in the words. He only prayed that people understood how he was mistreated, misunderstood, and abused by those closest to him. He wrote, yet he was left with crumbs. He smiled slightly at how much it hurt. There was no one quite like him, but he felt like he wasn't alone. For the first time, he wrote a story where he wasn't alone. No, he couldn't have been the only one. Or maybe he was. Only the page would tell.

He cried and covered his eyes so the tears didn't hit the page. Instead, his tears were ink. But he cried on the wooden table. They poured from his eyes. He just wanted it to end, but never wanted it to end. A human, he was all too human; even if you detest this man, his is Man, he is human, and detest him all you want, he sheds tears like you and has suffered just as much. All your indignities he's felt. All your misunderstandings, he'd been through and felt the brunt of. He'd been alone on his journey just like you.

Don't give this villain anything, for he is a killer. But if you feel even a bit, give him sympathy. If you can't sympathize with this young, dry child, then understand that he'd been orphaned young and alienated early.

Rich? Yes.

But he gave away his gold just to be stabbed in the back again.

Oh! It's the gift that keeps on giving! I cry for my son, lost and alone.

Good people are worth more than gold—people that care and cry with you. Therefore, with no people who cried or cared, he was the poorest of all the commoners. Let him burn, I guess.

Chapter 19

The Dreams Of A Streetsweeper

Kitan heard the same voice he heard every day, screeching in his ear, echoing all the time, ringing in his ears at night.

"No. Like this…. No! No! It goes like this!"

"I *was* doing that."

"*Don't* talk back to me, *boy*. I showed you how to do it."

"But I thought I was doing exactly that."

"No, no, no. You're scraping the street. You must *sweep* it. Let the broom do the work. You're only a dirty boy who makes messes. The broom gives your hands its purpose. It cleans everything... *if* you let it! You need to let it sweep and not get in its way."

"Like this?"

"Kind of like that. But easier. Softer! Easier! Let the sweeper do the work. You are only a tool for the broom. The sweeping is the purpose. You are only a tool. Remember that."

"So like this?"

"Kind of. You'll get it one day. But for now, realize what my mentor always taught me—these sweepers are the saviors for our streets, our only purpose. *Your* only purpose. You need to let the broom guide you. You have nothing without the broom. Your hands are a tool. Your mind.... Your mind is only meant to give the broom meaning."

"So I give the broom life as a tool? I am—"

The older man smacked the boy in the mouth with his whole arm. He whipped the boy again in the cheek with his big hand. The boy felt sick from yet another beating.

"You are the tool! This broom is your life. You will keep hold of it and let it do the work for you."

Kitan gasped for air as his head pounded with pain and his cheek felt tender and soft with blood. There was no one around to save him. He looked down at the dirty sidewalk. It seemed to be a canvas for all his failures. He watched the dust blow in the wind. But all the countless particles he could never sweep away were his job, and he failed miserably at that job as he trained in pain.

"But the broom was created by human hands and human minds. I don't see how it is only a tool, where I breathe life into it, making it useful to help society be cleaner and healthier.

The boy looked up for one quick second, one second long enough to see the furious eyes of the man, yellowed in pain. Before he got knocked out, his last glimpse was a giant arm swinging like a whip. It hit his cheek, and he saw stars as he fell to the ground. Only black and tiny lights dappling like sparks. His vision went dark with stars. Sprinkles of light showed in his head as he fell to the hard ground like a small tree. They struck him hard in the head. Saucers of light and dots of bright stars spackled his blurry vision. He would never know the trauma that one hit caused or the many hits after that.

Stars in a black night.

The boy groaned and scrambled to his feet after some time and asked another question. His body was drained of pain and fear. He didn't cry. His lungs stretched for air after the beating. "Please, please, Sir... I onlyhavahhquestion...."

"And I have an answer. You sweep. That's my answer! You let the broom glide gently over the sidewalks until you die." The bigger, older, hairier man laughed at the little boy who could not fight back. His crooked smile singed a picture into Kitan's wicked mind. Most boys would've given up and submitted by then. "And when you die, you will be replaced by a bigger, stronger, more useful person. That is to say, um, you're useless. Once you die, your bigger replacement will serve society better. You should be ashamed of yourself. Again! Do it again! I won't leave until I know you have it." The man watched until the boy could finally sweep again. He barely moved with any intent, still dazed from the hits to his head. "Okay. Okay, that's *better*. That's a good little slave. *Slave*: keep doing that... and do it again. Yep, just like that. Just let the broom sweep—that's all there is to it. Your mom would be proud of you. You're just pathetic enough to not get killed."

The boy's eyes lit up, forgetting everything else, abandoning his broom and letting his broom clack onto the sidewalk with a thump and a whisper into the quiet empty night. "I had a mom? I *have a mother*?"

His boss after he'd been hit again so hard and with the ferocity of hell. "No. You have no one. You only have me. No one gave birth to you, *slave*." Then he yelled into the night with houses all around the street. "Slave! Sweep! Sweep harder! No, softer than that! Here, watch. Let the broom do the work. Let the broom do the work. See that? Just let the broom do the work."

On the ground, the boy's bruised eyes saw unclean dust and stars of dark nights—never myth—stories told. It was a boy with no beyond, no past that he knew, and no future. He held the broom and looked up at the sky—he saw nothing. He didn't see stars. He didn't see a reason to live, but he kept living.

Some sort of slave. That's all King Menizak willed, and to do what the king willed—no matter the suffering and punishment—was the right thing to do. He lay there and twitched and turned and covered his ears, eyes, and cheeks from further strikes. It was bear paws and vipers that struck his stomach. If he had eaten that day, he would have vomited. He kept getting beat over the years— his head, his gut, his crotch, his legs bruised and battered over the years. Some nights, he would go into his lonely home, spraying blood from his mouth. He fainted and fell asleep with the last thing he pictured: the angry eyes of the man.

The boy grew to resent his master. Quietly. He silently seethed over time, grinding his teeth every time he was commanded to do something. He hated every voice that told him what to do, every hand that pointed where he had to go, or every time it hit him. Over time, he kept his questions to himself. He bottled it all up, putting his ideas on display in little pictures drawn in the dirt or little models he made out of scrap pieces of clay. His imagination grew every night; when it got cold and dark, his horizon grew brighter with hopeful futures of new things, wider pastures of possibilities. He was the poorest person in the city. He maybe—possibly, likely—had a mind brighter than any of the gold the nobility hoarded and any jewel fixed to the king's crown. He may have been the perfect hero, the perfect villain, the best person to be born into the worst circumstances of bondage and poverty.

It was all a cycle that never suggested *an end*. It was all a mirage, an elucidation, an holuptrex to an end that defied itself over and repeatedly until the next chapter turned to do the same thing.

An abandoned boy beaten and left with no love, watched only by those that despised him. But he had *questions*—dreams and fantasies—that outlived the aimless, stupid lives of all who would ever read this. Even the boy who knew he was bigger than his job was too small to grip his ambitions for a long time. And he was beaten down and beaten down and beaten again. No good-doer could do a thing about the injustice because injustice was people, and wherever people gathered, the weak would get beat down. That was the story. No gods held any fine sight over the dark night where the weak were beaten and beaten again.

Kitan kept his thoughts to himself; otherwise, he was beaten senseless.

Kitan spoke less with every day and imagined more.

Every night he sat alone and bruised by tiny flame. He was sore when he finally sat down, too tired to lay. He would bury his face in his palms and sometimes wished that the flame by his bed would burn it all down—not only his hut and him, but the city and the people that ruled it.

He cried less as the years came and went. He asked fewer questions and did more sweeping until he was trained into a neat and nice submissive servant who only wished to do his job well. His master finally looked at him with approval. The street sweeper took his hold on the lone alleys. He believed in something but wasn't sure what that was. The crowds of people dusted everything up, and their footsteps and tired shouts would make the dirt that would settle again and again, night after night.

Kitan sat alone on his rickety bed one night after another endless day. He looked at the tiny walls of his hut like a cage. His body was exhausted from another full day's work, but his restless mind still couldn't find peace. His visions wished to fly free, but he didn't quite know if they could survive outside the cage that trapped them.

His mind went adrift every night before he drifted off to sleep to grand places where everything worked, everyone worked, and everyone smiled. But it seemed so far off, and so he was forced to stare into the wispy flame by his bed, casting meaningless shadows he grew to hate. He hated his boss. He hated his job! He hated his life! But… why hate anything? What was there to hate? But he kept a bubbling despise for all those imagined slights, those dreams he couldn't draw up and pay for, and all the people that looked down on him from places he could never climb up to.

No one ever taught him anything, but the bright mind noticed things and learned a great deal from the streets he swept. *But if there's a day tomorrow, why can I not take it and make it mine?*

Kitan thought he was the dumbest person in Idaza, even less useful than a broom he could barely use. *Those people must've known much more than him if they were always smiling with money in hand while he was broke and broken, making sure their sandals didn't get dirty.*

He only wanted out and up from his ragged hut. He only wished to be somewhere else where he could view hills from afar and people from a place way up.

He only saw the dirt in his dreams—just more grains of sand to sweep. Every night bled into sunrise's bleak curtain.

But over time, the boy learned to *love* to serve. He learned to love to clean. While his body swept every day, his mind drifted to different places and better things.

He wished for an end to it all and never expected it, keeping bright eyes every night as the flame dimmed to nightfall.

His cage started to feel comfortable and safe. But of course, he never asked for a life of safety.

Chapter 20

History Is Born From Ash

The palace crumbled. It looked like a dark sun from afar, too bright and hot to be so close to the world. The great flame ate all it could on its way to devouring the center of the once-great nation.

Equality was a lie told to generations and spun up by fake traditions for feeble humans to cling to when the void of great black fire crept in on their bright eyes; their hope for some imaginary future could never exist without some tether to a past they could all believe in.

Chapter 21

The Screams Of The Rich

Many bureaucrats burned. The nobility was no longer noble. Now, as they writhed and hollered helplessly in the red flame, they would soon no longer exist.

A thousand screams sounded out in the smoke, burning alive, yelling for the help they would never get.

All the people in the palace that escaped the wreckage were swiftly killed by the soldiers standing guard on the emperor's command.

So much life! So much vitality and beauty! It certainly made for a story to tell, and what a story it was.

Chapter 22

Coyote Sets The Story Straight

Coyote thought of his lost love, who bled so much before she burned. He could still hear her high-pitched screech ringing in his ears. He could still see the body when he blinked.

***

He still remembered the first time he saw her from afar. She was younger then, with keen eyes and a tough stance, selling bread to the masses, shouting at the people in the line and passersby. She was so motivated, always striving better than what she was born as. He loved that about her. He loved everything about her. Metzli, the bread seller, the merchant, the worker, the studious and beautiful girl who he'd always wanted. That frame, that work ethic, that ambition, that person with the long dark hair and keen eyes made him believe in beauty again.

When they first met, she kindled hopeful sparks within Coyote. As she lay dying, she was useful material for more sparks.

He used to love her. And now he loved nothing once again. He did it to himself. And the gods did that to him.

They laughed at him from their high perch. They carefully made a man that could do no right—Coyote, the silly-angry kid emperor.

Now, a person with pen and power sat in a dark room, writing the next narrative to pass onto the people. They took all his messages well. The masses embraced every word as long as it sounded nice enough. Coyote always made the words sound nice. Pretty words and gritty stories.

He thought back to the mother releasing her timid daughter into nature, knowing full well it would hurt her, scratch her, and possibly leave her child harmed. But that wasn't her idea—it was Coyote's constant stories that circulated the kingdom that influenced her to do that. That mother only wanted the best for her child. Coyote, from far away, convinced her that harm and perilous paths would be best for her children—but he really believed it. That's what formed him. And so it would go on that way. The people would read the same message told in all different stories. But this one might be different yet.

Going down to go up. The darkness of the pit made the colors brighter. Maybe it mattered. It was only a jumble of ink on a page, but it felt like vital blood of life.

"Maximus! Where are you?"

"Yes, sir?" Footsteps approached the door. A shadow covered the light that came through the cracked door.

"I have finished this next manuscript. Please produce it for the people. Make extra copies, too."

"Very well. It will be done. How many extra copies would you like?"

"A lot. Now, hurry and go."

Chapter 23

Laughter In The Flame

The brittle remains of the royal palace simmered on the ground. Gray smog filled the city with a thick stench. The clouds hung low, blotting out the sun. All was gray and stripped and burned, sizzling as it burped out dying breaths. The great palace would only exist in memories and paintings from then on.

The commoners of Idaza—who far outnumbered the tiny number of nobles—saw the smoke and stared from afar. They all seemed to freeze at a sight they'd never seen. Quiet. Shivering. Numb eyes filled with smoke all faced toward the center of the kingdom, surrounding what once was the palace. Fear loomed large in their heavy chests. There were some old people that prayed to the sky for answers. Many young infants cried and quivered as their small pink lungs coughed up smoke. Some vomited in the thick stench. Parents grabbed their children's hands and rushed them indoors.

It was a gray mess of nothing and no action, only watching—the whole world watching, seeing if violence would break out in such a dismal sight—the gray billows of the great fire blotting out the sun. Their rulers and decision-makers were... in distress? Fighting? Was their emperor dead? They had to wait for answers.

Coughing. Silence for the whole city.

The city had never been so serene in its moribund cloud of gray, seeming to stay forever.

****

But night fell upon them all; it always did around this time. The whole city was blanketed in black, serenaded by the cries of the creatures of the night.

The black night sky covered the gray smog. The smoke wasn't thick enough to blot out the dark death of day.

The commoners whispered to their children. Husbands and wives argued in hushed voices. Nervous eyes looked out windows. Elderly folks hunched their shoulders and looked down at the floor, shaking their heads—even *they* had never seen anything like this over their many decades of living. Those adults had seen generations come and go in a stable nation; they didn't recognize what was happening after dark still, and so their hearts were gripped with fear.

Some children cried; some children hid in their rooms under the covers. Some yelled at their parents, and some parents yelled at each other.

No armed guards ever came. No burly men in red or black with spiteful pikes of death ever ravaged the commons. No soldiers came and kept people inside their homes. Instead, it was messengers, not soldiers, who made their way through the quiet streets in peace. They all came in droves and bowed their heads solemnly carrying great bundles of scrolls as was usual for this time of week and this time of week.

As the quiet settled down, the people burst out of their houses by the thousands to receive the messages brought to them. They needed the news. They hoped they would get an explanation.

One by one, by the thousands, the people came out of their houses and huts to receive the scrolls of the emperor's regular stories. They grasped for the scrolls as if it were their only drink after trudging through the desert over hot and dry days endless. They needed to make meaning out of this mess.

But the scrolls just told them to make their own meaning out of all of it. So many words for one simple message.

And they all—one by one—took the scrolls and read. But this time was different. Many laughed when they read the emperor's story. He told the truth. Was it a story if it happened? It had to be; that was the ultimate story.

He told them what he told them. He wrote true verses of his actions in the palace. He told his truest story, his adventures of attack and escape. Violence and innocence. What did it mean? Their emperor was really a murderer? It was the most grotesque story they had heard to this point. And it was true. Truth connected one line of dots through a galaxy of facts. That's all 'truth' is, and that's all it was to the people. Truth is both real and made up by the one who tells it.

The truth you're told is usually a lie.

One of them smiled, and another laughed. One of the neighbors heard them giggling after such a stressful afternoon. That neighbor also lightened her stride and softened her smile, waking a restful giant of laughter and celebration in the streets of Idaza. They had not heard the actual words of The Conjurer in so long—no more myths of ancient times, no more stories of the gods doing great things the normal people could never hope to do.

They love the written words of the emperor, who loved and lost and laughed and thought and cried like them. He was just like them! They could all relate to the emperor in all different ways. This was a person who did much wrong and follied his way through a life of confusion and suffering. They were just like him. They hated and laughed just like him.

They laughed because they knew they were ruled by a *human*, and even the sad stories he told them were good in the end because it was a man they could get to know, even if they could never understand him. And they laughed at the Valley of Death as they all grinned by nightfall, shining moon. They all lit countless crackling fires. Small patches of smoke showed up all around the city, small gatherings of family, friends, and newcomers who just wanted to sit and be beside people that laughed with each other. They weren't all friends. They weren't all family. They were just separated groups all together and laughing, telling the story told to them, talking about it, smiling in the night, knowing it might not be okay one day, but that was okay with them. More fires popped up all around the city like tiny suns in the night. Fires shown bright by the hundreds, and then by the thousands.

Laughing and dancing gave way to independent parties outside. All the surprise campfires made the black sky a little brighter, and the nighttime woes a little less bleak. Everyone with heavy burdens in their hearts felt a little lighter that night.

One of the gatherings got a little loud and rowdy, and a flaming torch struck a straw with a spark and lit a single home on fire. Yes, a home began to burn, but as people around noticed, it was put out quickly by a group of adults. They didn't know whose house it was, and so they left the burnt roof there and went back to their fires. At least there were no mosquitoes.

Blazes of blue and red coughed up crackling sparks that shot to the glowing moon. The sky stayed purely silent, and the emperor's many scrolls passed down to them were used as more kindling for the fire. It only made the flames hungrier. It all blazed bright. The many campfires defied the night sky and made enough light to blot out the stars.

The people laughed and danced together, and instruments could be heard all throughout the streets playing proudly, loudly enough for even lost souls of the nether realm to hear. The words were burned but not forgotten.

A few children stepped on hot cinders and started to cry in panic. A few more houses caught sparks and were set ablaze. But the chaos was controlled, fires were put out, and the pain was processed. It all worked—the pain and the sweating stressed bodies quivering in confused joy on their own—together and separately alone.

A great many lights in the clean streets burned brighter than the stars above, dancing with life and the will of the people. Every grin lit by every flame showed a constellation of teeth unique from the next. All the mouthpieces of the old kingdom screamed their own song, the one that celebrated their pain or paid homage to the dead and dying, or a sad song that spread hope or hopeless songs that spelled the most beautiful script.

The stars above were so pale and tired next to the people below who partied, sang their songs of sorrow and joy, and spread their light greater than any fleeting comet. No, this plane, these people; they were each larger than a star and felt more power than even those forces that created them. Maybe a whole life of pain was worth a moment of joy.

For then, right there, in the black and bleary sky, they told their own stories. They made statues and then crushed those statues, and history was what they made it, as was the future. Whatever got the city to that point was preserved in word but destroyed by flame.

Each person that night felt a twang that took to the tips of their fingers, the skin of their scalps, and the hard bones of their vertebrae in spastic sparks. They were imbued by their own selves, by each other, but then only on their lonesome, as they all gave birth to something new that night. So much pain for so many generations, from stone to marble and then to ash and flying dust, back to flame, the pain of birth subsided as the new being emerged for all those warmed by the blazing fires.

And thus, the individual was born.

Lights. Joy. Frigid ignorance in the void. The immense tragedy of the self, the futility of the future, the sorrow and indignities of isolation and cold loneliness, the hopeful spark of a new day, and the vigorous strength of a broken heart looking out on yet another pink sunrise, the regrets of the past and the guilt of the flesh, the triumph of the will, and the sagacious nature of feeling alive and only alive because what you eat does not nourish another, and what you take for yourself is for no one else. The individual lets up for no obstacle and lives, only lives, truly with either regret or shamelessness, unabashed in the face of pain.

Maybe it mattered.

Maybe it would all burn down, *and* if it ever did, what would arise from the ashes?

Chapter 24

An Old Friend Tells A Timeless Tale

An old man with a weathered face took a seat in a wicker chair with a groan. His smile was slow and warm. The children sat with their legs crossed on the floor, facing away from the old man. They all looked upon an orange beam cast by a torch, and the light on the empty wall ahead seemed to gaze back at all of them.

Silence came over the children as they all hushed each other with bright eyes. They jittered in place, waiting for something to happen—for something dark to clash with the light, signaling the start of a story.

They waited. They fidgeted.

A cough. A sniffle. Rustling and more jittering. One child shushed another as they all sat on the floor for the show to start.

And then a shadow overtook the orange light and was stenciled into the shape of some great building or cityscape.

"There was a time long ago…." The raspy man's voice sounded in the deathly quiet room.

And as the words of the man changed, and as his story took shape with his characters and events, so did the shadows on the wall. His voice with the shadows told a new tale for willing ears about a kingdom that sank into sorrow, a group of children that got lost, and the many dangers they met along the way. Monster faces with fangs and brave soldiers with spears, fighting then running, losing loved ones along the way, and feeling that sorrow on every step forward, wanting to turn back as the endless desert drew nearer.

He continued with his story as the children sat in awe of every word and shape that shifted in the light. They jumped at the sight of the monsters and clenched their fists when the characters fought, hearts beating a little quicker.

One child locked her hands together and raised them up to the light. "And then a giant eagle swooped in to fight the monster!" The shadow of a bird flapped its wings and descended into battle. The eagle howled and screeched.

"They all threw rocks at the beast!" Another boy tossed loose coins in the air in front of the light as a hailstorm of pellets flew down onto the shadow of the beast.

The tale continued, and the old man played along and grinned at his playful audience; they all wanted to be a part of the story; that was the whole point.

Time passed, and the children settled back down throughout the epic journey with the characters they connected with. It seemed like they all lived a lifetime watching the show, listening to the voices and the droning shadows that would live in their hearts and minds forever.

"And at long last, they found what they were looking for. Through loss and tiresome sorrow, they prevailed past all the trials that came their way, and the flame lived on forever."

The audience clapped and smiled and fidgeted as excited children often do. Their bright eyes sang with hope, all suggesting different things as soon as the story ended. They all asked questions as to what would happen next. They all desired different outcomes—after all, an audience was only a bunch of individuals.

"Again!"

"Another one!"

"Again!"

"What if they failed?"

"Tell another one!"

"Why did my favorite have to die at the end?"

The old man with the weathered face coughed a bit before speaking again, quieting the room again.

"If you would like another story or a tale told your own way, then go tell it yourself. Tell your own story with your whole heart and be proud you did it."

***

The children all ran off with minds open to the far-flung future, hearts welling with the richness of possibility in their new spirits. But one child stayed behind, perhaps unmoved by his peers' reaction to the epic tale they all witnessed by light of the flame. He sulked and stayed behind as the other kids all scurried away talking about ideas or just wanting to play a different game.

The old man saw the child standing and looking down at his feet. His brow wrinkled. "Hey."

The boy shook out of his trance and widened his eyes for a moment. "Hi."

"What troubles you?"

"What?"

"Is there something wrong?"

He shook his head. The orange candlelight in the room projected a shadow of the boy that loomed large and wavered over both of them like a dark giant.

"Did you enjoy the story?"

"Yes. Yeah, I really liked the story."

"And it seemed like all your friends did too. And yet, you don't share in their excitement. What is it?"

"Well… I guess I'm just not excited to tell stories that much. To sell stories. Make them. Make people believe them. I like watching them... hearing them. I just don't really want to act them out or tell them or write them like you did and like *they* want to do." He pointed outside to all the children running around.

"You're not interested in telling stories?" The old man hummed to himself and bobbed his head. "Then live one. Your life will be your story. You can make it as grand as you like."

"But monsters are fake. I'm not brave, and I can't be a soldier or a brave warrior in some fantasy story. I'm not going on a big adventure. I know exactly where my home is, and I know my parents, and I just do schoolwork like I'm told. I'm not a hero. I'm not like, well, I'm just not a hero." The boy looked down at his feet again and kicked a few specks of dust into the air that floated like snowflakes. "I don't have a story…. And I guess if I did, it'd be boring. No one's going to—"

"Woah! *Everyone* has a story. And it's in the small details of every day, made up of decisions that seem meaningless, that make the story what it is. Everything you do is worth it, and if you do it well enough, I'm sure it would make for a great tale."

The boy stared straight down. "I guess so. But I don't care if I'm remembered or if I do anything well. I'm not going to slay a dragon or anything like that. I don't really care if my life is remembered by people who don't know me. It's like everything that happens can be said in a million ways."

The man cleared his throat and sharpened his voice. "If you don't care about tales told from long ago or far into the future, then go—go live your own story. Make it all you can. There will always be more to say, but you can only do so much. So do it. Do it! And by all means, do it well. If something doesn't seem to matter to you, then make it matter, or find something that does."

"So what's my purpose, then?"

The old man grinned. His old eyes looked like hopeful sparks. "That's for you to find out. It's a part of your story."

"How will I know when I find my purpose?"

"Only you can know that."

And the child left confused and wishful, feeling alone under the giants of the night, the goliath of the days to come, towered over by the tasks at hand and the decisions to make—all too much to bear for any mind. He had grand stories in his mind and only dirt to look at.

When the boy left the old man, they were both alone—one a sedentary, smiling storyteller living out the rest of his days on a wicker chair, and the other off on the adventure for the rest of his life.

The old man sat back and listened to the careful silence of the quelling flame and the quiet of the closing night. He smiled at the thought of a boy who felt uninspired and confused, looking forward to a life he never asked for in a world he didn't understand.

The boy murmured to himself on his way back to his home just down the way. "*Monsters aren't real.*"

Monsters aren't real.... Monsters aren't real.

He repeated this to himself all the way back home until he fell asleep safely in the comfort of his sheets and pillows. He had troubling dreams that night of deep, echoing voices in a cavernous room from which he could not escape, equipped with nothing, nakedly in terror of the yellow eyes he saw so vividly that his mind conjured up without his consent.

He faced fanged creatures by himself in the nightmare as the dark forces descended upon him. His adventure was afoot, and the danger of life's precious gift teetered on a fine razor's edge.

He had a story to live. He would let others tell it.

Epilogue

And it was me all along, my own doing, my own meaning, or lack thereof. I told this story—I delivered you to the rarified heights where the air is thin, crisp, and cold, but I have also made you see the burgundy blood of the dying. I was there for every stabbing as you smelled the steaming blood of another human.

And the cycle will go on and stay that way, from critic to critic, old back down to young, and then old again, as it always has and always will. But I alone am immortal, for a shadow cannot be killed.

What I've drawn up is not some play or imaginative state in which you are free to frolic for a while like a child. No. I expect more from you, my *thinking* audience, so that you may one day see the obsidian sheen for what it truly is, for you—who you truly may be.

But maybe all I did was feed you another feeble story, just another dream to dream amidst a market of flashing headlines all begging for your eyes and attention.

Maybe you feel fooled and angry right now, hearing a *man* (ugh! A *male adult*) speak from above you as though he has grasped something you cannot reach. And then again, those that conjure creations live forever, so long as they continue to spread and grow.

But if you meet some unfortunate fate (and you *will)* and find the strength to face your own monsters while the whole world passes you by, not ever caring about the courage you needed to conquer while you took up your sword to craft your own journey, then, well, your journey is just that: another life among trillions before you and after you. And you may be fine and happy with how you so slayed the demons that sought to drag you down without ever having to tell a soul about it. But then, my friend, that trauma, that bravery, that kindness, that virtue in the tempest of suffering at Hell's own hot gate is your own and *only* your own, by your lonesome self with a story to tell and a weak and anxious pen still. If the word of your own life never reaches an ear or an eye, then ask yourself what good it may be and what good it may have done.

If no tales are told, then you have no story, just a life that dimmed as soon as that beacon flashed at its brightest.

But I just give the audience what they want, because that's all I want to do.

Your light in the dark labyrinth of life,

Mikalla

Nick Oliveri

More by Nick Oliveri

The Conjurer

Becoming The Conjurer

Monsters in My Mind

Her

Oxycodone And Her Canvas

A Boy Just Like Me

The Last Conjurer

Life's a Rip-off: A Book of Poetry

About The Author

Nick Oliveri is a Ukrainian-born, #1 bestselling author and fashion designer. He is often dubbed as a controversial creator of transgressive fiction and genre-bending literature.

Nick plumbs the depths of the human psyche in his fiction, sharing his potent tales of tragedy and triumph with the world. Skilled at crafting sentences that bring his characters and their narratives to life, he is passionate about the beauty the written word has to offer.

Oliveri draws from a unique set of creators that have inspired him throughout the years. These include Jean-Michel Basquiat, Vladimir Nabokov, Stephen King, Lil Wayne, and Hunter S. Thompson.

Nick is a former startup co-founder dedicated to the onset of the circular economy. Born in Ukraine but having grown up in the United States, today you can find Nick next to nowhere, and sometimes somewhere, enjoying whatever it is that he does.

Storiesofshadowandflame.com
Instagram: @nick0liveri
X/Twitter: @faultyharb

331

A Letter From The Conjurer